KU-775-857

CONFUSION

STEFAN ZWEIG

CONFUSION

THE PRIVATE PAPERS OF
PRIVY COUNCILLOR R VON D

Translated from the German by
Anthea Bell

PUSHKIN PRESS
LONDON

Pushkin Press,
71-75 Shelton Street,
London WC2H 9JQ

First published in German as
Verwirrung der Gefuehle in 1927
© William Verlag A G Zurich

English translation © Anthea Bell 2002

First published by Pushkin Press in 2002
Revised edition printed in 2009
This edition printed in 2013

ISBN 978 1 901285 22 2

All rights reserved. No part of this publication may be reproduced,
stored in a retrieval system or transmitted in any form or by any
means, electronic, mechanical, photocopying, recording or otherwise,
without prior permission in writing from Pushkin Press

Frontispiece: Stefan Zweig
© Roger-Viollet Rex Features

Set in 10.5 on 13.5 Monotype Baskerville

Proudly bound in Great Britain,
by TJ International Ltd, Padstow, Cornwall
and printed on Munken Premium White 90gsm

www.pushkinpress.com

CONFUSION

THEY MEANT WELL, my students and colleagues in the Faculty: there it lies, solemnly presented and expensively bound, the first copy of the Festschrift dedicated to me by the members of the Department of Languages and Literature on the occasion of my sixtieth birthday and to mark my thirty years of academic teaching. It is nothing short of a complete biographical record: no minor essay of mine has been overlooked, no ceremonial address, no trifling review in the annual volume of some learned journal or other has failed to be exhumed from its papery grave by bibliographical industry—my entire career up to the present day is set out with impeccable clarity, step by step like a well-swept staircase—it would be truly ungrateful of me to take no pleasure in this touching diligence. What I myself had thought lost, spent and gone, returns to me united and well-ordered in the form presented here: no, I cannot deny that as an old man I now scan these pages with the same pride as did the schoolboy whose report from his teachers first indicated that he had the requisite ability and strength of mind for an academic career.

And yet: when I had leafed through the two hundred industrious pages and looked my intellectual reflection in the eye, I couldn't help smiling. Was that really my life, did it truly trace as purposeful a course with such ease, from the first to the present day, as the biographer describes, sorting the paper records into order? I felt exactly as I did when I first heard my own voice on a recording: initially I did not recognize it at all, for it was indeed my voice but only as others hear it, not as I hear it myself through my blood and within my very being, so to speak. And so I, who have spent a lifetime depicting human beings in the light of their work, portraying the intrinsic intellectual structure of their worlds, was made aware again from my own experience of the impenetrability in every human life of the true core of its being, the malleable cell from which all growth proceeds. We live through myriads of seconds, yet it is always one, just one, that casts our entire inner world into turmoil, the second when (as Stendhal has described it) the internal inflorescence, already steeped in every kind of fluid, condenses and crystallizes—a magical second, like the moment of generation, and like that moment concealed in the warm interior of the individual life, invisible, untouchable, beyond the reach of feeling, a secret experienced alone. No algebra of the mind can calculate it, no alchemy of premonition divine it, and it can seldom perceive itself.

The book says not a word about this most secret factor in my mental development: that was why I couldn't help smiling. Everything it says is true—only what genuinely matters is missing. It merely describes me, it says nothing real about me. It speaks of me, but does not reveal what I am. The carefully compiled index comprises two hundred names—and the only one missing is the name of the man from whom all my creativity derived, who determined the course my life would take, and now calls me back to my youth with redoubled force. The book covers everything else, but not the man who gave me the gift of language and with whose tongue I speak: and suddenly I feel to blame for this craven silence. I have spent my life painting portraits of human beings, interpreting figures from past centuries for the benefit of today's sensibilities, and never thought of turning to the picture of the one most present to my mind. As in Homeric days, then, I will give that beloved shade my own blood to drink, so that he may speak to me again, and although he grew old and died long ago, be with me now that I too am growing old. I will add a page not previously written to those on open display, a confession of feelings to be set beside that scholarly book, and for his sake I will tell myself the true story of my youth.

BEFORE BEGINNING, I leaf once again through the book which claims to depict my life. And once again I cannot help smiling. How did they think they could reach the true core of my being when they chose to approach it in the wrong way? Even their very first step is wide of the mark! A former schoolmate, well disposed towards me and also a bearer of the honorary title of Privy Councillor, claims that even at grammar school my passion for the humanities distinguished me from all the other pupils. Your memory is at fault, my dear Privy Councillor! As far as I was concerned, anything in the way of humanist studies represented coercion which I could barely endure; I ground my teeth and fumed at it. For the very reason that, as the son of a headmaster in our small North German town, I was familiar at home with education as a means of earning a living, I hated everything to do with languages and literature from childhood: Nature, true to her mystic task of preserving the creative instinct, always impels the child to reject and despise its father's inclinations. Nature does not want weak, conformist progeny, merely continuing from where the previous generation left off: she always sets those of a kind at loggerheads, allowing the later-born to return to the ways of their forefathers only after making a laborious but fruitful detour. My father had only to venerate scholarship for my self-assertive instinct to regard it as mere intellectual sophistry; he praised the classics as a model to be followed, so they seemed to me didactic and I hated them. Surrounded by books, I despised them; with my father constantly pressing intellectual pursuits on me, I felt furious dislike for every kind of knowledge passed on by written tradition; it was not surprising, therefore, that I barely scraped through my school-leaving examinations and then vigorously resisted any idea of continuing my studies. I wanted to be an army officer, or join the navy, or be an engineer, although I had no really compelling inclination for any of those professions. Only my distaste for the papery didacticism of scholarship made me wish for a practical and active rather than an academic career. But my father, with his fanatical veneration for universities and everything to do with them, insisted on my following a course of academic studies, and the only concession I could win was permission to choose English as my subject rather than classics (a compromise which I finally accepted with the private reservation that a knowledge of English, the language of the sea, would make it easier for me later to adopt the naval career I so fervently desired).

Nothing could be further from the truth in that curriculum vitae of mine, then, than the well-meant statement that thanks to the guidance of meritorious professors I grasped the basic principles of the study of the arts in my first term—what did my passion for liberty, now impetuously breaking out, care then for lectures and lecturers? On my first brief visit to the lecture hall its stuffy atmosphere and the lecture itself, delivered in a monotonously clerical and self-important drone, so overcame me with weariness that it was an effort not to put my head down on the desk and doze off. Here I was back at the school I had thought myself so happy to escape, complete with classroom, teacher's lectern in an excessively elevated position, and quibbling pedantry—I could not help feeling as if sand were running out of the thin-lipped open mouth of the Privy Councillor addressing us, so steadily did the words of the worn lecture notebook drop into the thick air. The suspicion I had entertained even as a schoolboy that I had entered a morgue of the spirit, where uncaring hands anatomized the dead, was revived to an alarming degree in this factory churning out second-hand Alexandrian philosophy—and how intensely did I feel that instinct of rejection the moment the lecture I had sat through with such difficulty was over, and I stepped out into the streets of the city, the Berlin of those days which, surprised by its own growth, was bursting with a virility too suddenly attained, sparks flying from all its stones and all its streets, while the feverishly vibrant pace of life forced itself irresistibly on everyone, and in its avid greed greatly resembled the intoxication of my own only recently recognized sense of virility. Both the city and I had suddenly emerged from a repressive petit bourgeois atmosphere of Protestant orderliness, and were plunged too rapidly into a new delirium of power and opportunity—both of us, the city and I, a young fellow starting out in life, vibrated like a dynamo with restlessness and impatience. I never understood and loved Berlin as much as I did then, for every cell in my being was crying out for sudden expansion, just like every part of that overflowing, warm human honeycomb—and where could the impatience of my forceful youth have released itself but in the throbbing womb of that heated giantess, that restless city radiating power? It grasped me and took me to itself, I flung myself into it, went down into its very veins, my curiosity rapidly orbiting its entire stony yet warm body—I walked its streets from morning to night, went out to the lakes, discovered its secret places: I was truly a man possessed as, instead of paying attention to my studies, I flung myself into the lively and adventurous business of exploration. In these excesses, however, I was simply obeying an idiosyncrasy of my own—incapable from childhood of doing two things at once, I immediately became emotionally blind to any other occupation; everywhere and at all times I have felt the same impulse to press forward along a single line, and even in my work today I tend to sink my teeth so doggedly into a problem that I will not let go until I feel I have entirely drained it of substance.

At that time in Berlin my sense of liberation was so powerfully intoxicating that I could not endure even the brief seclusion of the lecture hall or the constraint of my own lodgings; everything that did not bring adventure my way seemed a waste of time. Still wet behind the ears, only just out of leading strings, the provincial youth that I was forced himself to appear a grown man—I joined a fraternity, sought to give my intrinsically rather shy nature a touch of boldness, jauntiness, heartiness; I had not been in the place a week before I was playing the part of cosmopolitan man about town, and I learned, with remarkable speed, to lounge and loll at my ease in coffee-houses, a true *miles gloriosus*. This chapter of manhood of course included women—or rather '*girls*', as we called them in our student arrogance—and it was much to my advantage that I was a strikingly good-looking young man. Tall, slim, the bronzed hue of the sea coast still fresh on my cheeks, my every movement athletically supple, I had a clear advantage over the pasty-faced shop-boys, dried like herrings by the indoor air, who like us students went out every Sunday in search of prey in the dance-floor cafés of Halensee and Hundekehle (then still well outside the city). I would take back to my lodgings now a flaxen-haired, milky-skinned servant girl from Mecklenburg, heated by the dancing, before she went home from her day off, now a timid, nervous little Jewish girl from Posen who sold stockings in Tietz's—most of them easy pickings, to be had for the taking and passed on quickly to my friends. The anxious schoolboy I had been only yesterday, however, found the unsuspected ease of his conquests a heady surprise—my successes, so cheaply won, increased my daring, and gradually I came to regard the street merely as the hunting ground for these entirely undiscriminating exploits, which were a kind of sport to me. Once, as I was stalking a pretty girl along Unter den Linden and—by pure coincidence—I came to the university, I could not help smiling to think how long it was since I had crossed that august threshold. Out of sheer high spirits I and a like-minded friend went in; we just opened the door a crack, saw (and an incredibly ridiculous sight it seemed) a hundred and fifty backs bent over their desks and scribbling, as if joining in the litany recited by a white-bearded psalmodist. Then I closed the door again, let the stream of that dull eloquence continue to flow over the shoulders of the industrious listeners, and strode jauntily out with my friend into the sunny avenue. It sometimes seems to me that a young man never wasted his time more stupidly than I did in those months. I never read a book, I am sure I never spoke a sensible word or entertained a thought worth the name—instinctively I avoided all cultivated society, merely in order to let my recently aroused body savour all the better the piquancy of the new and hitherto forbidden. This self-intoxication, this waste of time in wreaking havoc on oneself, may come naturally to every strong young man suddenly let off the leash—yet my peculiar sense of being possessed by it made this kind of dissolute conduct dangerous, and nothing was more likely than that I would have frittered away my life entirely, or at least have fallen victim to a dullness of feeling, had not chance suddenly halted my precipitous mental decline.

That chance—and today I gratefully call it a lucky one—consisted in my father's being unexpectedly summoned to the Ministry in Berlin for the day, for a headmasters' conference. As a professional educationalist, he seized his chance to get a random sample of my conduct without previous notice, taking me unawares and by surprise. His tactics succeeded perfectly. As usual in the evening, I was entertaining a girl in my cheap student lodgings in the north of the city—access was through my landlady's kitchen, divided off from my room by a curtain—and entertaining her very intimately too when I heard a knock on the door, loud and clear. Supposing it was another student, I growled crossly: "Sorry, not at home." After a short pause, however, the knocking came again, once, twice, and then, with obvious impatience, a third time. Angrily, I got into my trousers to send the importunate visitor packing, and so, shirt half-open, braces dangling, barefoot, I flung the door open, and immediately, as if I had been struck in the face by a fist, I recognized my father's shape in the darkness outside. I could make out little more of his face in the shadows than the lenses of his glasses, shining in the reflected light. However, that shadowy outline was enough for the bold words I had already prepared to stick in my throat, like a sharp fishbone choking me; for a minute or so I stood there, stunned. Then—and a terrible moment it was!—I had to ask him humbly to wait in the kitchen for a few minutes while I tidied my room. As I have said, I didn't see his face, but I sensed that he knew what was going on. I sensed it from his silence, from the restrained manner in which, without giving me his hand, he stepped behind the curtain in the kitchen with a gesture of distaste. And there, in front of an iron stove smelling of warmed-up coffee and turnips, the old man had to stand waiting for ten minutes, ten minutes equally humiliating to both of us, while I bundled the girl out of bed and into her clothes, past my father, who was listening against his will, and so out of the house. He could not help noticing her footsteps, and the way the folds of the curtain swung in the draught of air as she hurried off, and still I could not bring the old man in from his demeaning place of concealment: first I had to remedy the disorder of the bed, which was all too obvious. Only then—and I had never in my life felt more ashamed—only then did I face him.

My father retained his composure in this difficult situation, and I still privately thank him for it. Whenever I wish to remember him—and he died long ago—I refuse to see him from the viewpoint of the schoolboy who liked to despise him as no more than a correcting machine, constantly carping, a schoolmaster bent on precision; instead, I always conjure up his picture at this most human of moments, when deeply repelled, yet restraining himself, the old man followed me without a word into the oppressive atmosphere of my room. He was carrying his hat and gloves and was about to put them down automatically, but then made a gesture of revulsion, as if reluctant to let any part of himself touch such filth. I offered him an armchair; he did not reply, merely warded off all contact with the objects in this room with a movement of rejection.

After standing there, turned away from me, for a few icy moments, he finally took off his glasses and cleaned them with deliberation, a habit of his which, I knew, was a sign of embarrassment; nor did it escape me that when he put them on again the old man passed the back of his hand over his eyes. He felt ashamed in my presence, and I felt ashamed in his; neither of us could think of anything to say. Secretly I feared that he would launch into a sermon, an eloquent address delivered in that guttural tone I had hated and derided ever since my schooldays. But—and I still thank him for it today—the old man remained silent and avoided looking at me. At last he went over to the rickety shelf where my textbooks stood and opened them—one glance must have told him they were untouched, most of their pages still uncut. "Your lecture notes!" This request was the first thing he had said. Trembling, I handed them to him, well knowing that the shorthand notes I had made covered only a single lecture. He looked rapidly through the two pages, and placed the lecture notes on the table without the slightest sign of agitation. Then he pulled up a chair, sat down, looked at me gravely but without any reproach in his eyes, and asked: "Well, what do you think about all this? What now?"

This calm question floored me. Everything in me had been strung up—if he had spoken in anger, I would have let fly arrogantly in return, if he had admonished me emotionally I would have mocked him. But this matter-of-fact question broke the back of my defiance: its gravity called for gravity in return, its forced calm demanded respect and a readiness to respond. What I said I scarcely dare remember, just as the whole conversation that followed is something I cannot write down to this day—there are moments of emotional shock, a kind of swelling tide within, which when retold would probably sound sentimental, certain words which carry conviction only once, in private conversation and arising from an unforeseen turmoil of the feelings. It was the only real conversation I ever had with my father, and I had no qualms about voluntarily humbling myself; I left all the decisions to him. However, he merely suggested that I might like to leave Berlin and spend the next semester studying at a small university elsewhere; he was sure, he said almost comfortingly, that from now on I would work hard to make up for my omissions. His confidence shook me; in that one second I felt all the injustice I had done the old man throughout my youth, enclosed as he was in cold formality. I had to bite my lip hard to keep the hot tears in my eyes from flowing. And he may have felt something similar himself, for he suddenly offered me his hand, which shook as it held mine for a moment, and then made haste to leave. I dared not follow him, but stood there agitated and confused, and wiped the blood from my lip with my handkerchief, so hard had I dug my teeth into it in order to control my feelings.

This was the first real shock that, at the age of nineteen, I experienced—without a word spoken in anger, it overthrew the whole grandiose house of cards I had built during the last three months, a house constructed out of masculinity, student debauchery and bragging. I felt strong enough to give up all lesser pleasures for the act of will demanded of me, I was impatient to turn my wasted abilities to intellectual pursuits, I felt an avid wish for gravity, sobriety, discipline and severity. It was now that I vowed myself entirely to study, as if to a monastic ritual of sacrifice, although unaware of the transports of delight awaiting me in scholarship, and never guessing that adventures and perils lie ready for the impetuous in that rarefied world of the intellect as well.

The small provincial town where, with my father's approval, I had chosen to spend the next semester was in central Germany. Its far-flung academic renown was in stark contrast to the sparse collection of houses surrounding the university building. I did not have much difficulty in finding my way to my alma mater from the railway station, where I left my luggage for the time being, and as soon as I was inside the university, a spacious building in the old style, I felt how much more quickly the inner circle closed here than in the bustling city of Berlin. Within two hours I had enrolled and visited most of the professors; the only one not immediately available was my professor of English language and literature, but I was told he could be found taking his class at around four in the afternoon.

Driven by impatience, reluctant to waste an hour, as eager now to embark on the pursuit of knowledge as I had once been to avoid it, and after a rapid tour of the little town—which was sunk in narcotic slumber by comparison with Berlin—I turned up at the appointed place punctually at four o'clock. The caretaker directed me to the door of the seminar room. I knocked. And thinking a voice inside had answered, I went in.

However, I had misheard. No one had told me to come in, and the indistinct sound I had caught was only the professor's voice raised in energetic speech, delivering an obviously impromptu address to a close-packed circle of about two dozen students who had gathered around him. Feeling awkward at entering without permission because of my mistake, I was going to withdraw quietly again, but feared to attract attention by that very course of action, since so far none of the hearers had noticed me. Accordingly I stayed near the door, and could not help listening too.

The lecture had obviously arisen spontaneously out of a colloquium or discussion, or at least that was what the informal and entirely random grouping of teacher and students suggested—the professor was not sitting in a chair which distanced him from his audience as he addressed them, but was perched almost casually on a desk, one leg dangling slightly, and the young people clustered around him in informal positions, perhaps fixed in statuesque immobility only by the interest they felt in hearing him. I could see that they must have been standing around talking when the professor suddenly swung himself up on the desk, and from this more elevated position drew them to him with words as if with a lasso, holding them spellbound where they were. It was only a few minutes before I myself, forgetting that I had not been invited to attend, felt the fascinating power of his delivery working on me like a magnet; involuntarily I came closer, not just to hear him but also to see the remarkably graceful, all-embracing movements of his hands which, when he uttered a word with commanding emphasis, sometimes spread like wings, rising and fluttering in the air, and then gradually sank again harmoniously, with the gesture of an orchestral conductor muting the sound. The lecture became ever more heated as the professor, in his animated discourse, rose rhythmically from the hard surface of desk as if from the back of a galloping horse, his tempestuous train of thought, shot through with lightning images, racing breathlessly on. I had never heard anyone speak with such enthusiasm, so genuinely carrying the listeners away—for the first time I experienced what Latin scholars call a *raptus*, when one is taken right out of oneself; the words uttered by his quick tongue were spoken not for himself, nor for the others present, but poured out of his mouth like fire from a man inflamed by internal combustion.

I had never before known language as ecstasy, the passion of discourse as an elemental act, and the unexpected shock of it drew me closer. Without knowing that I was moving, hypnotically attracted by a force stronger than curiosity, and with the dragging footsteps of a sleepwalker I made my way as if by magic into that charmed circle—suddenly, without being aware of it, I was there, only a few inches from him and among all the others, who themselves were too spellbound to notice me or anything else. I immersed myself in the discourse, swept away by its strong current without knowing anything about its origin: obviously one of the students had made some comment on Shakespeare, describing him as a meteoric phenomenon, which had made the man perched on the desk eager to explain that Shakespeare was merely the strongest manifestation, the psychic message of a whole generation, expressing, through the senses, a time turned passionately enthusiastic. In a single outline he traced the course of that great hour in England's history, that single moment of ecstasy which can come unexpectedly in the life of every nation, as in the life of every human being, a moment when all forces work together to forge a way strongly forward into eternity. Suddenly the earth has broadened out, a new continent is discovered, while the oldest power of all, the Papacy, threatens to collapse; beyond the seas, now belonging to the English since the Spanish Armada foundered in the wind and waves, new opportunities arise, the world has opened up, and the spirit automatically expands with it—it too desires breadth, it too desires extremes of good and evil; it wishes to make discoveries and conquests like the conquistadors of old, it needs a new language, new force. And overnight come those who speak that language, the poets, fifty or a hundred in a single decade, wild, boisterous fellows who do not, like the court poetasters before them, cultivate their little Arcadian gardens and versify on elegant mythological themes—no, they storm the theatre, they set up their standard in the wooden buildings that were once merely the scene of animal shows and bloodthirsty sports, and the hot odour of blood still lingers in their plays, their drama itself is a *Circus Maximus* where the wild beats of emotion fall ravenously on one another. These unruly and passionate hearts rage like lions, each trying to outdo the others in wild exuberance; all is permitted, all is allowed on stage: incest, murder, evildoing, crimes, the boundless tumult of human nature indulges in a heated orgy; as the hungry beasts once emerged from their cages, so do the inebriated passions now race into the wooden-walled arena, roaring and dangerous. It is a single outburst exploding like a petard, and it lasts for fifty years: a rush of blood, an ejaculation, a uniquely wild phenomenon prowling the world, seizing on it as its prey—in this orgy of power you can hardly hear individual voices or make out individual figures. Each strikes sparks off his neighbour, they learn and they steal from each other, they strive to outdo one another, to surpass each other's achievement, yet they are all only intellectual gladiators in the same festive games, slaves unchained and urged on by the genius of the hour. It recruits them from dark, crooked rooms on the outskirts of the city, and from palaces too: Ben Jonson, the mason's grandson; Marlowe, the son of a cobbler; Massinger, the offspring of an upper servant; Philip Sidney, the rich and scholarly statesman—but the seething whirlpool flings them all together; today they are famous, tomorrow they die, Kyd and Heywood in dire poverty, starving like Spenser in King Street, none of them living respectable lives, ruffians, whore-masters, actors, swindlers, but poets, poets, poets every one. Shakespeare is only at their centre, "the very age and body of the time", but no one has the time to mark him out, so stormy is the turmoil, so vigorously does work spring up beside work, so strongly does passion exceed passion. And as suddenly as it vibrantly arose that magnificent eruption of mankind collapses again, twitching; the drama is over, England exhausted, and for another hundred years the damp and foggy grey of the Thames lies dull upon the spirit again. A whole race has scaled the heights and depths of passion in a single onslaught, feverishly spewing the overflowing, frenzied soul from its breast—and there the land lies now, weary, worn out; pettifogging Puritanism closes the theatres and thus silences the impassioned language, the Bible alone is heard again, the word of God, where the most human word of all had made the most fiery confessions of all time, and a single ardent race lived for thousands in its own unique way.

And now, with a sudden change of direction, the dazzling discourse is turned on us: "So now do you see why I don't begin my course of lectures in chronological order, with King Arthur and Chaucer, but with the Elizabethans, in defiance of all the rules? And do you see that what I most want is for you to be familiar with them, get a sense of that liveliest of periods? One can't have literary comprehension without real experience, mere grammatical knowledge of the words is useless without recognition of their values, and when you young people want to understand a country and its language you should start by seeing it at its most beautiful, in the strength of its youth, at its most passionate. You should begin by hearing the language in the mouths of the poets who create and perfect it, you must have felt poetry warm and alive in your hearts before we start anatomizing it. That's why I always begin with the gods, for England is Elizabeth, is Shakespeare and the Shakespeareans, all that comes earlier is preparation, all that comes afterwards pale imitation of that true bold leap into infinity—but here, and you must feel it for yourselves, young people, here is the most truly alive youthfulness in the world. All phenomena, all humanity is to be recognized only in its fiery form, only in passion. For the intellect arises from the blood, thought from passion, passion from enthusiasm—so look at Shakespeare and his kind first, for they alone will make you young people genuinely young! Enthusiasm first, then diligence—enthusiasm giving you the finest, most extreme and greatest tutorial in the world, before you turn to studying the words.

"Well, that's enough for today—goodbye to you!" With an abrupt concluding gesture his hand rose in the air and imperiously descended again with an unexpected movement, and he jumped down from the desk at the same time. As if shaken apart, the dense crowd of students dispersed, seats creaked and banged, desks were pushed back, twenty hitherto silent throats suddenly began to speak, to clear themselves, to take a deep breath—only now did I realize how magnetic had been the spell closing all those living lips. The tumultuous discussion in that small space was all the more heated and uninhibited now; several students approached the lecturer with thanks, or some other comment, while the others exchanged impressions, their faces flushed, but no one stood by calmly, no one was left untouched by the electric tension, its contact now suddenly broken, yet its aura and its fire still seeming to crackle in the close air of the room.

I myself could not move—I felt I had been pierced to the heart. Of an emotional nature myself, unable to grasp anything except in terms of passion, my senses racing headlong on, I had felt carried away for the first time by another human being, a teacher; I had felt a superior force before which it was both a duty and a pleasure to bow. I felt the blood hot in my veins, my breath came faster, that racing rhythm throbbed through my body, seizing impatiently on every joint in it. Finally I gave way to instinct and slowly made my way to the front to see the man's face, for strange to say, as he spoke I had not perceived his features at all, so indistinct had they seemed, so immersed in what he was saying. Even now I could at first see only the indistinct outline of a shadowy profile; he was standing in the dim light by the window, half turning towards one of the students, hand laid in a friendly manner on his shoulder. Yet even that fleeting movement had an intimacy and grace about it which I would never have thought possible in an academic.

Meanwhile some of the students had noticed me, and to avoid appearing too much of an unwanted intruder I took a few more steps towards the professor and waited until he had finished his conversation. Only then did I see his face clearly: a Roman head, with a brow like domed marble, and a wave of hair cascading back, a shining white shock, bushy at the sides, the upper part of the face of an impressively bold and intellectual cast—but below the deeply shadowed eyes it was immediately made softer, almost feminine, by the smooth curve of the chin, the mobile lips with the nerves fluttering around the restless line of the sporadic smile. The attractive masculinity of the forehead was resolved by the more pliant lines of the flesh in the rather slack cheeks and mobile mouth; seen at close quarters his countenance, at first imposing and masterful, appeared to make up a whole only with some difficulty. His bearing told a similarly ambiguous story. His left hand rested casually on the desk, or at least seemed to rest there, for little tremors constantly passed over the knuckles, and the slender fingers, slightly too delicate and soft for a man's hand, impatiently traced invisible figures on the bare wooden surface, while his eyes, covered by heavy lids, were lowered in interest as he talked. Whether he was simply restless, or whether the excitement was still quivering in his agitated nerves, the fidgety movement of his hand contrasted with the quiet expectancy of his face as he listened; he seemed immersed in his conversation with the student, weary yet attentive.

At last my turn came. I approached him, gave him my name and said what I wanted, and at once his bright eyes turned on me, the pupils almost shining with blue light. For two or three full seconds of inquiry that glance traversed my face from chin to hairline; I may well have flushed under this mildly inquisitorial observation, for he answered my confusion with a quick smile. "So you want to enrol with me? Well, we must have a longer talk. Please forgive me, but I can't see to it at once; I have something else I must do, but perhaps you'll wait for me down by the entrance and walk home with me." So saying, he gave me his hand, a slender and delicate hand that touched my fingers more lightly than a glove, and then turned in a friendly manner to the next student.

I waited outside the entrance for ten minutes, my heart beating fast. What was I to say if he asked after my studies, how could I confess that I had never thought about poetry much in either my work or my hours of leisure? Would he not despise me, even exclude me without more ado from that ardent circle which had so magically surrounded me today? But no sooner did he appear, rapidly striding closer with a smile, than his presence dispelled all my awkwardness, and I confessed unasked (unable to conceal anything about myself from him) to the way in which I had wasted my first term. Yet again that warm and sympathetic glance dwelt on me. "Well, music has rests as well as notes," he said with an encouraging smile, and obviously intent on not shaming my ignorance further he turned to humdrum personal questions—where was my home, where was I going to lodge here? When I told him that I had not yet found a room he offered his help, suggesting that I might like to enquire first in the building where he himself lived; a half-deaf old lady had a nice little room to rent, and any of his students who took it had always been happy there. He'd see to everything else himself, he said; if I really showed that I meant what I said about taking my studies seriously, he would consider it a pleasant duty to help me in every way. On reaching his rooms he once again offered me his hand and invited me to visit him at home next evening, so that we could work out a programme of study for me together. So great was my gratitude for this man's unhoped-for kindness that I merely shook his hand respectfully, raised my hat in some confusion, and forgot to say even a word of thanks.

O F COURSE I immediately rented the little room in the same building. I would have taken it even if it had not appealed to me at all, solely for the naively grateful notion of being physically closer to this captivating man, who had taught me more in an hour than anyone else I had ever heard. But the room was charming anyway: on the attic floor above my professor's own lodgings, it was a little dark because of the overhanging wooden gables, and its window offered a panoramic view of the nearby rooftops and the church tower. There was a green square in the distance, and the clouds I loved at home sailed overhead. The landlady, a little old lady who was deaf as a post, looked after her lodgers with a touchingly maternal concern; I had come to an agreement with her within a couple of minutes, and an hour later I was hauling my suitcase up the creaking wooden stairs.

I did not go out that evening; I even forgot to eat or smoke. The first thing I did was to take the Shakespeare I happened to have packed out of my case and read it impatiently, for the first time in years. That lecture had aroused my passionate curiosity, and I read the poet's words as never before. Can one account for such transformations? A new world suddenly opened up on the printed page before me, the words moved vigorously towards me as if they had been seeking me for centuries; the verse coursed through my veins in a fiery torrent, carrying me away, inducing the same strange sense of relaxation behind the brow as one feels in a dream of flight. I shook, I trembled, I felt the hot surge of my blood like a fever—I had never had such an experience before, yet I had done nothing but listen to an impassioned lecture. However, the exhilaration of that lecture must have lingered on within me, and when I read a line aloud I heard my voice unconsciously imitating his, the sentences raced on in the same headlong rhythm, my hands felt impelled to move, arching in the air like his own—as if by magic, in a single hour, I had broken through the wall which previously stood between me and the world of the intellect, and passionate as I was by nature, I had discovered a new passion, one which has remained with me to the present day: a desire to share my enjoyment of all earthly delights in the inspired poetic word. By chance I had come upon Coriolanus, and as if reeling in a frenzy I discovered in myself all the characteristics of that strangest of the Romans: pride, arrogance, wrath, contempt, mockery, all the salty, leaden, golden, metallic elements of the emotions. What a new delight it was to divine and understand all this at once, as if by magic! I read on and on until my eyes were burning, and when I looked at the time it was three-thirty in the morning. Almost alarmed by this new force which had both stirred and numbed my senses for six hours on end, I put out the light. But the images still glowed and quivered within me; I could hardly sleep with longing for the next day and looking forward to it, a day which was to expand the world so enchantingly opened up to me yet further and make it entirely my own.

NEXT DAY, however, brought disappointment. My impatience had made me one of the first to arrive at the lecture hall, where my teacher (as I will call him from now on) was to speak on English phonetics. Even as he came in I received a shock—was this the same man as yesterday, or was it only my excited mood and my memory that had made him a Coriolanus, wielding words in the Forum like lightning, heroically bold, crushing, compelling? The figure who entered the room, footsteps dragging slightly, was a tired old man. As if a shining but opaque film had been lifted from his countenance I now saw, from where I was sitting in the front row of desks, his almost unhealthily pallid features, furrowed by deep wrinkles and broad crevices, with blue shadows wearing channels away in the dull grey of his cheeks. Lids too heavy for his eyes shadowed them as he read his lecture, and the mouth, its lips too pale, too thin, delivered the words with no resonance: where was his merriment, where were the high spirits rejoicing in themselves? Even the voice sounded strange, moving stiffly through grey, crunching sand at a monotonous and tiring pace, as if sobered by the grammatical subject.

I was overcome by restlessness. This was not the man I had been waiting for since the early hours of the morning—where was the astrally radiant countenance he had shown me yesterday? This was a worn-out professor droning his way objectively through his subject; I listened with growing anxiety, wondering whether yesterday's tone might return after all, the warmly vibrant note that had struck my feelings like a hand playing music, moving them to passion. Increasingly restless, I raised my eyes to him, full of disappointment as I scanned that now alien face: yes, this was undeniably the same countenance, but as if emptied, drained of all its creative forces, tired and old, the parchment mask of an elderly man. Were such things possible? Could a man be so youthful one minute and have aged so much the next? Did such sudden surges of the spirit occur that they could change the countenance as well as the spoken word, making it decades younger?

The question tormented me. I burned within, as if with thirst, to know more about the dual aspect of this man, and as soon as he had left the rostrum and walked past us without a glance, I hurried off to the library, following a sudden impulse, and asked for his works. Perhaps he had just been tired today, his energy muted by some physical discomfort, but here, in words set down to endure, I would find the key to his nature, which I found so curiously challenging, and the way to

42

approach it. The library assistant brought the books; I was surprised to find how few there were. So in twenty years the ageing man had published only this sparse collection of unbound pamphlets, prefaces, introductions, a study of whether or not Pericles was genuinely by Shakespeare, a comparison between Hölderlin and Shelley (this admittedly at a time when neither poet was regarded as a genius by his own people)—and apart from that mere odds and ends of literary criticism? It was true that all these works announced a forthcoming two-volume publication: *The Globe Theatre: History, Productions, Poets*—but the first mention of it was dated two decades ago, and when I asked again the librarian confirmed that it had never appeared. Rather hesitantly, with only half my mind on them, I leafed through these writings, longing for them to revive that powerful voice, that surging rhythm. But these works moved at a consistently measured pace; nowhere did I catch the ardently musical rhythm of his headlong discourse, leaping over itself as wave breaks over wave. What a pity, something sighed within me. I could have kicked myself, I felt so angry and so suspicious of the feelings I had too quickly and credulously entertained for him.

But I recognized him again in that afternoon's class. This time he did not begin by speaking himself. Following the custom of English college debates the students, a couple of dozen of them, were divided into those supporting the motion and those opposing it. The subject itself was from his beloved Shakespeare, namely, whether Troilus and Cressida (from his favourite work) were to be understood as figures of burlesque: was the work itself a satyr play, or did its mockery conceal tragedy? Soon what began as mere intellectual conversation became electrical excitement and took fire, with his skilful hand fanning the flames—forceful argument countered claims made casually, sharp and keen interjections heated the discussion until the students were almost at loggerheads with each other. Only once the sparks were really flying did he intervene, calming the overexcited atmosphere and cleverly bringing the debate back to its subject, but at the same time giving it stronger intellectual stimulus by moving it surreptitiously into a timeless dimension—and there he suddenly stood amidst the play of these dialectical flames, in a state of high excitement himself, both urging on and holding back the clashing opinions, master of a stormy wave of youthful enthusiasm which broke over him too. Leaning against the desk, arms crossed, he looked from one to another, smiling at one student, making a small gesture encouraging another to contradict, and his eyes shone with as much excitement as yesterday. I felt he had to make an effort not to take the words out of their mouths. But he restrained himself—by main force, as I could tell from the way his hands were pressed more and more firmly over his breast like the stave of a barrel, as I guessed from the mobile corners of his mouth, which had difficulty in suppressing the words rising to his lips. And suddenly he could do it no longer, he flung himself into the debate like a swimmer into the flood—raising his hand in an imperious gesture he halted the tumult as if with a conductor's baton; everyone immediately fell silent, and now he summed up all the arguments in his own vaulting fashion. And as he spoke the countenance he had worn yesterday re-emerged, wrinkles disappeared behind the flickering play of nerves, his throat arched, his whole bearing was bold and masterful, and abandoning his quiet, attentive attitude he flung himself into the talk as if into a torrent. Improvisation carried him away—now I began to guess that, sober-minded in himself, when he was teaching a factual subject or was alone in his study he lacked that spark of dynamite which here, in our intense and breathlessly spellbound company, broke down his inner walls; he needed—oh yes, I felt it—he needed our enthusiasm to kindle his own, our receptive attitude for his own extravagance, our youth for his own rejuvenated fervour. As a player of the cymbals is intoxicated by the increasingly wild rhythm of his own eager hands, his discourse became ever grander, ever more ardent, ever more colourful as his words grew more fervent, and the deeper our silence (I could not help feeling that we were all holding our breath in that room) the more elevated, the more intense was his performance, the more did it sound like an anthem. In those moments we were all entirely his, all ears, immersed in his exuberance.

Yet again, when he suddenly ended with a quotation from Goethe on Shakespeare, our excitement impetuously broke out. Yet again he leaned against the desk exhausted, as he had leaned there yesterday, his face pale but with little runs and trills of the nerves twitching over it, and oddly enough the afterglow of the sensuality of release gleamed in his eyes, as if in a woman who has just left an overpowering embrace. I felt too shy to speak to him now, but by chance his glance fell on me. And obviously he sensed my enthusiastic gratitude, for he smiled at me in a friendly manner, and leaning slightly towards me, hand on my shoulder, reminded me to go to see him that evening as we had agreed.

I was at his door at seven o'clock precisely, and with what trepidation did I, a mere boy as I was, cross that threshold for the first time! Nothing is more passionate than a young man's veneration, nothing more timid, more feminine than its uneasy sense of modesty. I was shown into his study, a semi-twilit room in which the first things I saw, looking through the glass panes over them, were the coloured spines of a large number of books. Over the desk hung Raphael's *School of Athens*, a picture which (as he told me later) he particularly loved, because all kinds of teaching, all forms of the intellect are symbolically united here in perfect synthesis. I was seeing it for the first time, and instinctively I thought I traced a similarity to his own brow in the highly individual face of Socrates. A figure in white marble gleamed behind me, an attractively scaled-down bust of the Paris *Ganymede*, and beside it there was a *St Sebastian* by an old German master, tragic beauty set, probably not by chance, beside its equivalent enjoying life to the full. I waited with my heart beating fast, as breathless as all the nobly silent artistic figures around me; they spoke to me of a new kind of intellectual beauty, a beauty that I had never suspected and that still was not clear to me, although I already felt prepared to turn to it with fraternal emotion. But I had no time to look around me, for at this point the man I was waiting for came in and approached me, once again showing me that softly enveloping gaze, smouldering like a hidden fire, and to my own surprise thawing out the most secret part of me. I immediately spoke as freely to him as to a friend, and when he asked about my studies in Berlin the tale of my father's visit suddenly sprang to my lips—I took fright even as I spoke of it—and I assured this stranger of my secret vow to devote myself to my studies with the utmost application. He looked at me, as if moved.

Then he said: "Not just with application, my boy, but above all with passion. If you do not feel impassioned you'll be a schoolmaster at best—one must approach these things from within and always, always with passion." His voice grew warmer and warmer, the room darker and darker. He told me a great deal about his own youth, how he too had begun foolishly and only later discovered his own inclinations—I must just have courage, he said, and he would help me as far as lay within him; I must not scruple to turn to him with any questions, ask anything I wanted to know. No one had ever before spoken to me with such sympathy, with such deep understanding; I trembled with gratitude, and was glad of the darkness that hid my wet eyes.

I could have spent hours there with him, taking no notice of the time, but there was a soft knock on the door. It opened, and a slender, shadowy figure came in. He rose and introduced the newcomer. "My wife." The slender shadow came closer in the gloom, placed a delicate hand in mine, and then said, turning to him: "Supper's ready." "Yes, yes, I know," he replied hastily and (or so at least it seemed to me) with a touch of irritation. A chilly note suddenly seemed to have entered his voice, and when the electric light came on he was once again the ageing man of that sober lecture hall, bidding me good night with a casual gesture.

I SPENT THE NEXT TWO WEEKS in a passionate frenzy of reading and learning. I scarcely left my room, I ate my meals standing up so as not to waste time, I studied unceasingly, without a break, almost without sleep. I was like that prince in the Oriental fairy tale who, removing seal after seal from the doors of locked chambers, finds more and more jewels and precious stones piled in each room and makes his way with increasing avidity through them all, eager to reach the last. In just the same way I left one book to plunge into another, intoxicated by each of them, never sated by any: my impetuosity had moved on to intellectual concerns. I had a first glimmering of the trackless expanses of the world of the mind, which I found as seductive as the adventure of city life had been, but at the same time I felt a boyish fear that I would not be up to it, so I economized on sleep, on pleasures, on conversation and any form of diversion merely so that I could make full use of my time, which I had never felt so valuable before. But what most inflamed my diligence was vanity, a wish to come up to my teacher's expectations, not to disappoint his confidence, to win a smile of approval, I wanted him to be conscious of me as I was conscious of him. Every fleeting occasion was a test; I was constantly spurring my clumsy but now curiously inspired mind on to impress and surprise him; if he mentioned an author with whom I was unfamiliar during a lecture, I would go in search of the writer's works that very afternoon, so that next day I could show off by parading my knowledge in the class discussion. A wish uttered in passing which the others scarcely noticed was transformed in my mind into an order; in this way a casual condemnation of the way students were always smoking was enough for me to throw away my lighted cigarette at once, and give up the habit he deplored immediately and for ever. His words, like an evangelist's, bestowed grace and were binding on me too; I was always on the qui vive, attentive and intent upon greedily snapping up every chance remark he happened to drop. I seized on every word, every gesture, and when I came home I bent my mind entirely to the passionate recapitulation and memorizing of what I had heard; my impatient ardour felt that he alone was my guide, and all the other students merely enemies whom my aspiring will urged itself daily to outstrip and outperform.

Either because he sensed how much he meant to me, or because my impetuosity appealed to him, my teacher soon distinguished me by showing his favour publicly. He gave me advice on what to read, although I was a newcomer to the class he brought me to the fore in general debate in an almost unseemly manner, and I was often permitted to visit him for a confidential talk in the evening. On these occasions he would usually take a book down from the shelf and read aloud in his sonorous voice, which always rose an octave and grew more resonant when he was excited. He read from poems and tragedies, or he explained controversial cruxes; in those first two weeks of exhilaration I learned more of the nature of art than in all my previous nineteen years. We were always alone during this evening hour. Then, about eight o'clock, there would be a soft knock on the door: his wife letting him know that supper was ready. But she never again entered the room, obviously obeying instructions not to interrupt our conversation.

S O FOURTEEN DAYS had gone by, days crammed to the full, hot days of early summer, when one morning, like a steel spring stretched too taut, my ability to work deserted me. My teacher had already warned me not to overdo my industry, advising me to set a day aside now and then to go out and about in the open air—and now his prophecy was suddenly fulfilled: I awoke from a stupefied sleep feeling dazed, and when I tried to read I found that the characters on the page flickered and blurred like pinheads. Slavishly obeying every least word my teacher uttered, I immediately decided to follow his advice and take a break from the many days avidly devoted to my education in order to amuse myself. I set out that very morning, for the first time made a thorough exploration of the town, parts of which were very old, climbed the hundreds of steps to the church tower in the cause of physical exercise, and looking out from the viewing platform at the top discovered a little lake in the green spaces just outside town. As a coast-dwelling northerner, I loved to swim, and there on the tower, from which even the dappled meadows looked like shimmering pools of green water, an irresistible longing to throw myself into that beloved element again suddenly overcame me like a gust of wind blowing from my home. No sooner had I made my way to the swimming pool after lunch and begun splashing about in the water than my body began to feel at ease again, the muscles in my arms stretched flexibly and powerfully for the first time in weeks, and within half-an-hour the sun and wind on my bare skin had turned me back into the impetuous lad of the old days who would scuffle vigorously with his friends and venture his life in daredevil exploits. Striking out strongly, exercising my body, I forgot all about books and scholarship. Returning to the passion of which I had been deprived so long, in the obsessive way characteristic of me, I had spent two hours in my rediscovered element, I had dived from the board some ten times to release my strength of feeling as I soared through the air, I had swum right across the lake twice, and my vigour was still not exhausted. Spluttering, with all my tense muscles stretched, I looked around for some new test, impatient to do something notable, bold, high-spirited.

Then I heard the creak of the diving board from the nearby ladies' pool and felt the wood quivering as someone took off with strong impetus. Curving as it dived to form a steely crescent like a Turkish sword, the body of a slender woman rose in the air and came down again head first. For a moment the dive drove a splashing, foaming white whirlpool into the water, and then the taut figure reappeared, striking out vigorously for the island in the middle of the lake. "Chase her! Catch up with her!" An urge for athletic pleasure came over my muscles, and with a sudden movement I dived into the water and followed her trail, stubbornly maintaining my tempo, shoulders forging their way forward. But obviously noticing my pursuit, and ready for a sporting challenge herself, my quarry made good use of her start, and skilfully passed the island at a diagonal angle so that she could make her way straight back. Quickly seeing what she meant to do, I turned as well, swimming so vigorously that my hand, reaching forward, was already in her wake and only a short distance separated us—whereupon my quarry cunningly dived right down all of a sudden, to emerge again a little later close to the barrier marking off the ladies' pool, which prevented further pursuit. Dripping and triumphant, she climbed the steps and had to stop for a moment, one hand to her breast, her breath obviously coming short, but then she turned, and on seeing me with the barrier keeping me away gave a victorious smile, her white teeth gleaming. I could not really see her face against the bright sunlight and underneath her swimming cap, only the bright and mocking smile she flashed at me as her defeated opponent.

I was both annoyed and pleased: this was the first time I had felt a woman's appreciative glance on me since

Berlin—perhaps an adventure beckoned. With three strokes I swam back into the men's pool and quickly flung my clothes on, my skin still wet, just so that I could be in time to catch her coming out at the exit. I had to wait ten minutes, and then my high-spirited adversary—there could be no mistaking her boyishly slender form—emerged, stepping lightly and quickening her pace as soon as she saw me waiting there, obviously meaning to deprive me of the chance of speaking to her. She walked with the same muscular agility she had shown in swimming, with a sinewy strength in all her joints as they obeyed that slender, perhaps too slender body, a body like that of an ephebe; I was actually gasping for breath and had difficulty in catching up with her escaping figure as she strode out, without making myself conspicuous. At last I succeeded, swiftly crossed the path ahead of her at a point where the road turned, airily raising my hat in the student manner, and before I had really looked her in the face I asked if I could accompany her. She cast me a mocking sideways glance, and without slowing her rapid pace replied, with almost provocative irony: "Why not, if I don't walk too fast for you? I'm in a great hurry." Encouraged by her ease of manner, I became more pressing, asked a dozen inquisitive and on the whole rather silly questions, which she none the less answered willingly, and with such surprising freedom that my

56

intentions were confused rather than challenged. For my code of conduct when approaching a woman in my Berlin days was adjusted to expect resistance and mockery rather than frank remarks such as my interlocutor made while she walked rapidly along, and once again I felt I had shown clumsiness in dealing with a superior opponent.

But worse was to come. For when, more indiscreetly importunate than ever, I asked where she lived, two bright and lively hazel eyes were suddenly turned on me, and she shot back, no longer concealing her amusement: "Oh, very close to you indeed." I stared in surprise. She glanced sideways at me again to see if her Parthian shot had gone home. Sure enough, it had struck me full in the throat. All of a sudden my bold Berlin tone of voice was gone; very uncertainly, indeed humbly, I asked, stammering, whether my company was a nuisance to her. "No, why?" she smiled again. "We have only two more streets to go, we can walk them together." At that moment my blood was in turmoil, I could scarcely go any further, but what alternative did I have? To walk away would have been even more of an insult, so I had to accompany her to the building where I lodged. Here she suddenly stopped, offered me her hand, and said casually: "Thank you for your company! You'll be seeing my husband at six this evening, I expect."

I must have turned scarlet with shame. But before I could apologize she had run nimbly upstairs, and there I stood, thinking with horror of the artless remarks I had so foolishly and audaciously made. Boastful idiot that I was, I had invited her to go on a Sunday outing as if she were some little seamstress, I had paid indirect compliments to her physical charm, then launched into sentimental complaints of the life of a lonely student—my self-disgust nauseated me so much that I was retching with shame. And now she was going off to her husband, full of high spirits, to tell him about my foolishness—a man whose opinion meant more to me than anyone's. I felt it would be more painful to appear ridiculous to him than to be whipped round the market square naked in public.

I passed dreadful hours until evening came: I imagined, a thousand times over, how he would receive me with his subtle, ironic smile—oh, I knew he was master of the art of making a sardonic comment, and could sharpen a jest to such keen effect that it drew blood. A condemned man could not have climbed the scaffold with a worse sensation of choking than mine as I climbed the stairs, and no sooner did I enter his room, swallowing a large lump in my throat with difficulty, than my confusion became worse than ever, for I thought I had heard the whispering rustle of a woman's dress in the next room. My high-spirited acquaintance must be in there listening, ready to relish my embarrassment and enjoy the discomfiture of a loud-mouthed young man. At last my teacher arrived. "What on earth's the matter with you?" he asked, sounding concerned. "You look so pale today." I made some non-committal remark, privately waiting for the blow to fall. But the execution I feared never came; he talked of scholarly subjects, just the same as usual: not a word contained any ironic allusion, anxiously as I listened for one. And first amazed, then delighted, I realized that she had said nothing.

At eight o'clock the usual knock on the door came. I said goodnight with my heart in my throat again. As I went out of the doorway she passed me: I greeted her, and her eyes smiled slightly at me. My blood flowing fast, I took this forgiveness on her part as a promise that she would keep silent in the future too.

F ROM THEN ON I BECAME ATTENTIVE in a new way; hitherto, my boyish veneration of the teacher whom I idolized had seen him so much as a genius from another world that I had entirely omitted to think of his private, down-to-earth life. With the exaggeration inherent in any true enthusiasm, I had imagined his existence as remote from all the daily concerns of our methodically ordered world. And just as, for instance, a man in love for the first time dares not undress the girl he adores in his thoughts, dares not think of her as a natural being like the thousands of others who wear skirts, I was disinclined to venture on any prying into his private life: I knew him only in sublimated form, remote from all that is subjective and ordinary. I saw him as the bearer of the word, the embodiment of the creative spirit. Now that my tragicomic adventure had suddenly brought his wife across my path, I could not help observing his domestic and family life more closely; indeed, although against my will, a restless, spying curiosity was aroused within me. And no sooner did this curiosity awaken than it became confused, for on his own ground his was a strange, an almost alarmingly enigmatic existence. The first time I was invited to a family meal, not long after this encounter, and saw him not alone but with his wife, I began to suspect that they had a strange and unusual relationship, and the further I subsequently made my way into the inner circle of his home, the more confusing did this feeling become. Not that any tension or sense that they were at odds made itself felt in word or gesture: on the contrary, it was the absence of any such thing, the lack of any tension at all between them that enveloped them both so strangely and made their relationship opaque, a heavy silence of the feelings, like the heaviness of the *föhn* wind when it falls still, which made the atmosphere more oppressive than a stormy quarrel or lightning flashes of hidden rancour. Outwardly, there was nothing to betray any irritation or tension, but their personal distance from each other could be felt all the more strongly. In their odd form of conversation, question and answer touched only briefly, as it were, with swift fingertips, and never went wholeheartedly along together hand in hand. Even their remarks to me were hesitant and constrained at mealtimes. And sometimes, until we returned to the subject of work, the conversation froze entirely into a great block of silence which in the end no one dared to break. Its cold weight would lie oppressively on my spirit for hours.

His total isolation horrified me more than anything. This man, with his open, very expansive disposition, had no friends of any kind; his students alone provided him with company and comfort. No relationship but correct civility linked him to his university colleagues, he never attended social occasions; often he did not leave home for days on end to go anywhere but the twenty steps or so it took him to reach the university. He buried everything silently within him, entrusting his thoughts neither to any other human being nor to writing. And now, too, I understood the volcanic, fanatically exuberant nature of his discourse in his circle of students—after being dammed up for days his urge to communicate would break out, all the ideas he carried silently within him rushed forth, with the uncontrollable force known to horsemen when a mount is fresh from the stable, breaking out of the confines of silence into this headlong race of words.

At home he spoke very seldom, least of all to his wife. It was with anxious, almost ashamed surprise that even I, an inexperienced young man, realized that there was some shadow between these two people, in the air and ever present, the shadow of something intangible that none the less cut them off completely from one another, and for the first time I guessed how many secrets a marriage hides from the outside world. As if a pentagram were traced on the threshold, his wife never ventured to enter his study without an explicit invitation, a fact which clearly signalled her complete exclusion from his intellectual world. Nor would my teacher ever allow any discussion of his plans and his work in front of her; indeed, I found it positively embarrassing to hear him abruptly break off his passionate, soaring discourse the moment she came in. There was even something almost insulting and manifestly contemptuous, devoid of civility, in his brusque and open rejection of any interest she showed—but she appeared not to be insulted, or perhaps she was used to it. With her lively, boyish face, light and agile in her movements, supple and lithe, she flew upstairs and downstairs, was always busy yet always had time for herself, went to the theatre, enjoyed all kinds of athletic sports—but this woman aged about thirty-five took no pleasure in books, in the domestic life of the household, in anything abstruse, quiet, thoughtful. She seemed at ease only when—always warbling away, laughing easily, ready for bantering conversation—she could move her limbs in dancing, swimming, running, in some vigorous activity; she never spoke to me seriously, but always teased me as if I were an adolescent boy; at the most, she would accept me as a partner in our high-spirited trials of strength. And this swift and light-hearted manner of hers was in such confusingly stark contrast to my teacher's dark and entirely withdrawn way of life, which could be lightened only by some intellectual stimulus, that I kept wondering in amazement what on earth could have brought these two utterly different natures together. It was true that this striking contrast did me personally nothing but good; if I fell into conversation with her after a strenuous session of work, it was as if a helmet pressing down on my brow had been removed; the ecstatic ardour was gone, life returned to the earthly realm of clear, daylight colours, cheerfulness playfully demanded its dues, and laughter, which I had almost forgotten in my teacher's austere presence, did me good by relieving the overwhelming pressure of my intellectual pursuits. A kind of youthful camaraderie grew up between her and me; and for the very reason that we always spoke casually of unimportant matters, or went to the theatre together, there was no tension at all in our relationship. Only one thing—awkwardly, and always confusing me—interrupted the easy tenor of our conversations, and that was any mention of his name. Here my probing curiosity inevitably met with an edgy silence on her part, or when I talked myself into a frenzy of enthusiasm with a strangely enigmatic smile. But her lips remained closed on the subject: she shut her husband out of her life as he shut her out of his, in a different way but equally firmly. Yet the two of them had lived together for fifteen years under the same secluded roof.

The more impenetrable this mystery, the more it appealed to my passionate and impatient nature. Here was a shadow, a veil, and I felt its touch strangely close in every draught of air; sometimes I thought myself close to catching it, but its baffling fabric would elude me, only to waft past me again next moment, never becoming perceptible in words or taking tangible form. Nothing, however, is more arousing and intriguing to a young man than a teasing set of vague suspicions; the imagination, usually wandering idly, finds its quarry suddenly revealed to it, and is immediately agog with the newly discovered pleasure of the chase. Dull-minded youth that I had been, I developed entirely new senses at this time—a thin-skinned membrane of the auditory system that caught every give-away tone, a spying, avid glance full of keen distrust, a curiosity that groped around in the dark—and my nerves stretched elastically, almost painfully, constantly excited as they apprehended a suspicion which never subsided into a clear feeling.

But I must not be too hard on my breathlessly intent curiosity, for it was pure in nature. What raised all my senses to such a pitch of agitation was the result not of that lustful desire to pry which loves to track down base human instincts in someone superior—on the contrary, that agitation was tinged with secret fear, a puzzled and hesitant sympathy which guessed, with uncertain anxiety, at the suffering of this silent man. For the closer I came to his life the more strongly was I oppressed by the almost three-dimensional deep shadows on my teacher's much-loved face, by that noble melancholy—noble because nobly controlled—which never lowered itself to abrupt sullenness or unthinking anger; if he had attracted me, a stranger, on that first occasion by the volcanic brilliance of his discourse, now that I knew him better I was all the more distressed by his silence and the cloud of sadness resting on his brow. Nothing has such a powerful effect on a youthful mind as a sublime and virile despondency: Michelangelo's *Thinker* staring down into his own abyss, Beethoven's mouth bitterly drawn in, those tragic masks of suffering move the unformed mind more than Mozart's silver melody and the radiant light around Leonardo's figures. Being beautiful in itself, youth needs no transfiguration: in its abundance of strong life it is drawn to the tragic, and is happy to allow melancholy to suck sweetly from its still inexperienced bloom, and the same phenomenon accounts for the eternal readiness of young people to face danger and reach out a fraternal hand to all spiritual suffering.

And it was here that I became acquainted with the face of a man genuinely suffering in such a way. The son of ordinary folk, growing up in safety and bourgeois comfort, I knew sorrow only in its ridiculous everyday forms, disguised as anger, clad in the yellow garment of envy, clinking with trivial financial concerns—but the desolation of that face, I felt at once, derived from a more sacred element. This darkness was truly of the dark; a pitiless pencil, working from within, had traced folds and rifts in cheeks grown old before their time. Sometimes when I entered his study (always with the timidity of a child approaching a house haunted by demons) and found him so deep in thought that he failed to hear my knock, when suddenly, ashamed and dismayed, I stood before his self-forgetful figure, I felt as if it were only Wagner sitting there, a physical shell in Faust's garment, while the spirit roamed mysterious chasms, visiting sinister ceremonies on Walpurgis Night. At such moments his senses were entirely sealed away; he heard neither an approaching footstep nor a timid greeting. Then, suddenly recollecting himself, he would start up and try to cover the awkwardness: he would walk up and down and try to divert my observant glance away from him by asking questions. But the darkness still shadowed his brow for a long time, and only his ardent discourse could disperse those clouds gathering from within.

He must sometimes have felt how much the sight of him moved me, perhaps he saw it in my eyes, my restless hands, perhaps he suspected that a request for his confidence hovered unseen on my lips, or recognized in my tentative attitude a secret longing to take his pain into myself. Yes, surely he must feel it, for he would suddenly interrupt his lively conversation and look at me intently, and indeed the curious warmth of his gaze, darkened by its own depth, would pour over me. Then he would often grasp my hand, holding it restlessly for some time—and I always expected: now, now, now he is going to talk to me. But instead there was usually a brusque gesture, sometimes even a cold, intentionally deflating or ironic remark. He, who was enthusiasm itself, who nourished and aroused it in me, would suddenly strike it away from me as if marking a mistake in a poorly written essay, and the more he saw how receptive to him I was, yearning for his confidence, the more curtly would he make such icy comments as: "You don't see the point," or: "Don't exaggerate like that," remarks which angered me and made me despair. How I suffered from this man who moved from hot to cold like a bright flash of lightning, who unknowingly inflamed me, only to pour frosty water over me all of a sudden, whose exuberant mind spurred on my own, only to lash me with irony—I had a terrible feeling that the closer I tried to come to him, the more harshly, even fearfully he repelled me. Nothing could, nothing must approach him and his secret.

For I realized more and more acutely that secrecy strangely, eerily haunted his magically attractive depths. I guessed at something unspoken in his curiously fleeting glance, which would show ardour and then shrink away when I gratefully opened my mind to him; I sensed it from his wife's bitterly compressed lips, from the oddly cold, reserved attitude of the townspeople, who looked almost offended to hear praise of him—I sensed it from a hundred oddities and sudden moments of distress. And what torment it was to believe myself in the inner circle of such a life, and yet to be wandering, lost as if in a labyrinth, unable to find the way to its centre and its heart!

However, it was his sudden absences that I found most inexplicable and agitating of all. One day, when I was going to his lecture, I found a notice hanging up to say that there would be no classes for the next two days. The students did not seem surprised, but having been with him only the day before I hurried home, afraid he might be ill. His wife merely smiled dryly when my impetuous entrance betrayed my agitation. "Oh, this happens quite often," she said, in a noticeably cold tone. "You just don't know about it yet." And indeed the other students told me that he did indeed disappear overnight like this quite often, sometimes simply telegraphing an apology; one of them had once met him at four in the morning in a Berlin street, another had seen him in a bar in a strange city. He would rush off all at once like a cork popping out of a bottle, and on his return no one knew where he had been. His abrupt departure upset me like an illness; I went around absent-mindedly, restlessly, nervously for those two days. Suddenly my studies seemed pointlessly empty without his familiar presence, I was consumed by vague and jealous suspicions, indeed I felt something like hatred and anger for his reserve, the way he excluded me so utterly from his real life, leaving me out in the cold like a beggar when I so ardently wished to be close to him. In vain did I tell myself that as a boy, a mere student, I had no right to demand explanations and ask him to account for himself, when he was already kind enough to give me a hundred times more of his confidence than his duty as a university teacher required. But reason had no power over my ardent passion—ten times a day, foolish boy that I was, I asked whether he was back yet, until I began to sense bitterness in his wife's increasingly brusque negatives. I lay awake half the night and listened for his homecoming step, and in the morning I lurked restlessly close to his door, no longer daring to ask. And when at last and unexpectedly he entered my room on the third day I gasped—my surprise must have been excessive, or so at least I saw from its reflection in the embarrassed displeasure with which he asked a few hasty, trivial questions. His glance avoided mine. For the first time our conversation went awkwardly, one comment stumbling over another, and while we both carefully avoided any reference to his absence, the very fact that we were ignoring it prevented any open discussion. When he left me my curiosity flared up like a fire—it came to devour my sleeping and waking hours.

M Y EFFORTS TO FIND ELUCIDATION and deeper understanding lasted for weeks—I kept obstinately making my way towards the fiery core I thought I felt volcanically active beneath that rocky silence. At last, in a fortunate hour, I succeeded in making my first incursion into his inner world. I had been sitting in his study once again until twilight fell, as he took several Shakespearean sonnets out of a locked drawer and read those brief verses, lines that might have been cast in bronze, first in his own translation, then casting such a magical light on their apparently impenetrable cipher that amidst my own delight I felt regret that everything this ardent spirit could give was to be lost in the transience of the spoken word. And suddenly—where I got it from I do not know—I found the courage to ask why he had never finished his great work on *The History of the Globe Theatre*. But no sooner had I ventured on the question than I realized, with horror, that I had inadvertently and roughly touched upon a secret, obviously painful wound. He rose, turned away, and said nothing for some time. The room seemed suddenly too full of twilight and silence. At last he came towards me, looked at me gravely, his lips quivering several times before they opened slightly, and then painfully made his admission: "I can't tackle a major work. That's over now—only the young make such bold plans. I have no stamina these days. Oh, why hide it? I've become capable only of brief pieces; I can't see anything longer through. Once I had more strength, but now it's gone. I can only talk—then it sometimes carries me away, something takes me out of myself. But I can't work sitting still, always alone, always alone."

His resignation shattered me. And in my fervent conviction I urged him to reconsider, to record in writing all that he so generously scattered before us daily, not just giving it all away but putting his own thoughts into constructive form. "I can't write now," he repeated wearily, "I can't concentrate enough." "Then dictate it!" I cried, and carried away by this idea I urged, almost begged him: "Dictate it to me. Just try! Perhaps only the beginning—and then you may find you can't help going on. Oh, do try dictating, I wish you would—for my sake!"

He looked up, first surprised, then more thoughtful. The idea seemed to give him food for thought. "For your sake?" he repeated. "You really think it could give anyone pleasure for an old man like me to undertake such a thing?" I felt him hesitantly beginning to yield, I felt it from his glance, a moment ago turned sadly inward, but now, softened by warm hope, gradually looking out and brightening. "You really think so?" he repeated; I already felt a readiness streaming into his mind, and then came an abrupt: "Then let's try! The young are always right, and is wise to do as they wish." My wild expressions of delight and triumph seemed to animate him: he paced rapidly up and down, almost youthfully excited, and we agreed that we would set to work every evening at nine, immediately after supper—for an hour a day at first. We began on the dictation next evening.

How can I describe those hours? I waited for them all day long. By afternoon a heavy, unnerving restlessness was weighing electrically on my impatient mind; I could scarcely endure the hours until evening at last came. Once supper was over we would go straight to his study, I sat at the desk with my back turned to him while he paced restlessly up and down the room until he had got into his rhythm, so to speak, until he raised his voice and launched into the prelude. For this remarkable man constructed it all out of his musicality of feeling: he always needed some vibrant note to set his ideas flowing. Usually it was an image, a bold metaphor, a situation visualized in three dimensions which he extended into a dramatic scene, involuntarily working himself up as he went rapidly along. Something of all that is grandly natural in creativity would often flash from the swift radiance of these improvisations: I remember lines that seemed to be from a poem in iambic metre, others that poured out like cataracts in magnificently compressed enumerations like Homer's catalogue of ships or the barbaric hymns of Walt Whitman. For the first time it was granted to me, young and new to the world as I was, to glimpse something of the mystery of the creative process—I saw how the idea, still colourless, nothing but pure and flowing heat, streamed from the furnace of his impulsive excitement like the molten metal to make a bell, then gradually, as it cooled, took shape, I saw how that shape rounded out powerfully and revealed itself, until at last the words rang from it and gave human language to poetic feeling, just as the clapper gives the bell its sound. And in the same way as every single sentence rose from the rhythm, every description from a picturesquely visualized image, so the whole grandly constructed work arose, not at all in the academic manner, from a hymn, a hymn to the sea as infinity made visible and perceptible in earthly terms, its waves reaching from horizon to horizon, looking up to heights, concealing depths—and among them, with crazily sensuous earthly skill, ply the tossing vessels of mankind. Using this maritime simile in a grandly constructed comparison, he presented tragedy as an elemental force, intoxicating and destructively overpowering the blood. Now the wave of imagery rolls towards a single land—England arises, an island eternally surrounded by the breakers of that restless element which perilously encloses all the ends of the earth, every zone and latitude of the globe. There, in England, it sets up its state—there the cold, clear gaze of the sea penetrates the glassy housing of the eye, eyes grey and blue; every man is both a man of the sea and an island, like his own country, and strong, stormy passions, represented by the storms and danger of the sea, are present in a race that had constantly tried its own strength in centuries of Viking voyaging. But now peace lies like a haze over this land surrounded by surging breakers; accustomed to storms as they are, however, its people would like to go to sea again, they want headlong, raw events attended by daily danger, and so they re-create that rising, lashing tension for themselves in bloody and tragic spectacles. The wooden trestles are constructed for baiting animals and staging fights between them. Bears bleed to death, cockfights arouse a bestial lust for horror; but soon more elevated minds wish to draw a pure and thrilling tension from heroic human conflicts. Then, building on the foundations of religious spectacle and ecclesiastical mystery plays, there arises that other great and surging drama of humanity, all those adventures and voyages return, but now to sail the seas of the heart, a new infinity, another ocean with its spring tides of passion and swell of the spirit to be navigated with excitement, and to be ocean-tossed in it is the new pleasure of this later but still strong Anglo-Saxon race: the national drama of England emerges, Elizabethan drama.

And the formative word rang out, full-toned, as he launched himself with enthusiasm into the description of that barbarically primeval beginning. His voice, which at first raced along fast in a whisper, stretching muscles and ligaments of sound, became a metallically gleaming airborne craft pressing on ever more freely, ever further aloft—the room, the walls pressed close in answer, became too small for it, it needed so much space. I felt a storm surging over me, the breaking surf of the ocean's lip powerfully uttered its echoing word; bending over the desk, I felt as if I were standing among the dunes of my home again, with the great surge of a thousand waves coming up and sea spray flying in the wind. All the sense of awe that surrounds both the birth of a man and the birth of a work of literature broke for the first time over my amazed and delighted mind at this time.

If my teacher ended his dictation at the point where the strength of his inspiration tore the words magnificently away from their scholarly purpose, where thought became poetry, I was left reeling. A fiery weariness streamed through me, strong and heavy, not at all like his own weariness, which was a sense of exhaustion or relief, while I, over whom the storm had broken, was still trembling with all that had flowed into me.

Both of us, however, always needed a little conversation afterwards to help us find sleep or rest. I would usually read over what I had taken down in shorthand, and curiously enough, no sooner did my writing become spoken words than another voice breathed through my own and rose from it, as if something had transformed the language in my mouth. And then I realized that, in repeating his own words, I was scanning and forming his intonations with such faithful devotion that he might have been speaking out of me, not I myself—so entirely had I come to echo his own nature. I was the resonance of his words. All this is forty years ago, yet still today, when I am in the middle of a lecture and what I am saying breaks free from me and spreads its wings, I am suddenly, self-consciously aware that it is not I myself speaking, but someone else, as it were, out of my mouth. Then I recognize the voice of the beloved dead, who now has breath only on my lips; when enthusiasm comes over me, he and I are one. And I know that those hours formed me.

T HE WORK GREW, it grew around me like a forest, its shade gradually excluding any view of the outside world. I lived only in that darkness, in the work that spread wider and further, among the rustling branches that roared ever more loudly, in the man's warm and ambient presence.

Apart from my few hours of university lectures and classes, my whole day was devoted to him. I ate at their table, day and night messages passed upstairs and downstairs to and from their lodgings—I had their door key, and he had mine so that he could find me at any time of day without having to shout for our half-deaf old landlady. However, the more I became one with this new community, the more totally did I turn away from the outside world: I shared not only the warmth of this inner sphere but its frosty isolation. My fellow students, without exception, showed me a certain coldness and contempt—who knew whether some secret verdict had been passed on me, or just jealousy provoked by our teacher's obvious preference for me? In any case, they excluded me from their society, and in class discussions it seemed that they had agreed not to speak to me or offer any greeting. Even the other professors did not hide their hostility; once, when I asked the professor of Romance languages for some trivial piece of information, he fobbed me off ironically by saying: "Well, intimate as you are with Professor … , you should know that." I sought in vain to account to myself for such undeserved ostracism. But the words and looks I received eluded all explanation. Ever since I had been living on such close terms with that lonely couple, I myself had been entirely isolated.

This exclusion would have given me no further cause for concern, since my mind, after all, was entirely bent on intellectual pursuits, except that in the end the constant strain was more than my nerves could stand. You do not live for weeks in a permanent state of intellectual excess with impunity, and moreover in switching too wildly from one extreme to the other I had probably turned my whole life upside down far too suddenly to avoid endangering the equilibrium secretly built into us by Nature. For while my dissolute behaviour in Berlin had relaxed my body pleasantly, and my adventures with women gave playful release to dammed-up instincts, here an oppressively heavy atmosphere weighed so constantly on my irritated senses that they would only churn around in electrical peaks within me. I forgot how to enjoy deep, healthy sleep, although—or perhaps because—I was always up until the early hours of the morning copying out the evening's dictation for my own pleasure (and burning with puffed-up impatience to hand the written sheets to my beloved mentor at the earliest opportunity). Then my university studies and the reading through which I raced called for further preparation, and my condition was aggravated, not least, by my conversations with my teacher, since I strained every nerve in Spartan fashion so as never to appear to him in a poor light. My abused body did not hesitate to take revenge for these excesses. I suffered several brief fainting fits, warning signs that I was putting an insane strain on Nature—but my hypnotic sense of exhaustion increased, all my feelings were vehemently expressed, and my exacerbated nerves turned inward, disturbing my sleep and arousing confused ideas of a kind I had previously restrained.

The first to notice an obvious risk to my health was my teacher's wife. I had already seen her concerned glance dwelling on me, and she made admonitory remarks during our conversations with increasing frequency, saying, for instance, that I must not try to conquer the world in a single semester. Finally she spoke her mind. "Now that's enough," she said sharply one Sunday when I was working away at my grammar, while it was beautiful sunny weather outside, and she took the book away from me. "How can a lively young man be such a slave to ambition? Don't take my husband as your example all the time; he's old and you are young, you need a different kind of life." That undertone of contempt flashed out whenever she spoke of him, and devoted to him as I was it always roused me to indignation. I felt that she was intentionally, perhaps in a kind of misplaced jealousy, trying to keep me further away from him, countering my extreme enthusiasm with ironic comments. If we sat too long over our dictation in the evening she would knock energetically on the door, and force us to stop work in spite of his angry reaction. "He'll wear your nerves out, he'll destroy you completely," she once said bitterly on finding me in a state of exhaustion. "Look what he's reduced you to in just a few weeks! I can't stand by and watch you harming yourself any longer. And what's more … " She stopped, and did not finish her sentence. But her lip was quivering, pale with suppressed anger.

Indeed, my teacher did not make it easy for me: the more passionately I served him, the more indifferent he seemed to my eagerly helpful devotion. He rarely gave me a word of thanks; in the morning, when I took him the work on which I had laboured until late at night, he would say, dryly: "Tomorrow would have done." If my ambitious zeal outdid itself in offering unasked-for assistance, his lips would suddenly narrow in mid-conversation, and an ironic remark would repel me. It is true that if he then saw me flinch, humiliated and confused, that warmly enveloping gaze would be turned on me again, comforting me in my despair, but how seldom, how very seldom that was! And the way he blew hot and cold, sometimes coming so close as to cast me into turmoil, sometimes fending me off in annoyance, utterly confused my unruly feelings which longed—but I was never able to say clearly what it was I really longed for, what I wanted, what I required and aspired to, what sign of his regard I hoped for in my enthusiastic devotion. For if one feels reverent passion even of a pure nature for a woman, it unconsciously strives for physical fulfilment; nature has created an image of ultimate union for it in the possession of the body—but how can a passion of the mind, offered by one man to another and impossible to fulfil, ever find complete satisfaction? It roams restlessly around the revered figure, always flaring up to new heights of ecstasy, yet never assuaged by any final act of devotion. It is always in flux but can never flow entirely away; like the spirit, it is eternally insatiable. So when he came close it was never close enough for me, his nature was never entirely revealed, never really satisfied me in our long conversations; even when he cast aside all his aloofness I knew that the next moment some sharp word or action could cut through our intimacy. Changeable as he was, he kept confusing my feelings, and I do not exaggerate when I say that in my overexcited state I often came close to committing some thoughtless act just because his indifferent hand pushed away a book to which I had drawn his attention, or because suddenly, when we were deep in conversation in the evening and I was absorbing his ideas, breathing them all in, he would suddenly rise—having only just laid an affectionate hand on my shoulder—and say brusquely: "Off you go, now! It's late. Good night." Such trivialities were enough to upset me for hours, indeed for days. Perhaps my exacerbated feelings, constantly overstretched, saw insults where none were intended—although what use are explanations thought up to soothe oneself when the mind is so disturbed? But it went on day after day—I suffered ardently when he was close, and froze when he kept his distance, I was always disappointed by his reserve, he gave no sign to mollify my feelings, I was cast into confusion by every chance occurrence.

And oddly enough, whenever he had injured my sensitive feelings it was with his wife that I took refuge. Perhaps it was an unconscious urge to find another human being who suffered similarly from his silent reserve, perhaps just a need to talk to someone and find, if not help, at least understanding—at any rate, I resorted to her as if to a secret ally. Usually she mocked my sense of injury away, or said, with a cold shrug of her shoulders, that I should be used to his hurtful idiosyncrasies by now. Sometimes, however, when sudden desperation reduced me all at once to a quivering mass of reproaches, incoherent tears and stammered words, she would look at me with a curious gravity, with a glance of positive amazement, but she said nothing, although I could see movement like stormy weather around her lips, and I felt it was as much as she could do not to come out with something angry or thoughtless. She too, no doubt, would have something to tell me, she too had a secret, perhaps the same as his; but while he would repel me brusquely as soon as I said something that came too close, she generally avoided further comment with a joke or an improvised prank of some kind.

Only once did I come close to extracting some comment from her. That morning, when I took my teacher the passage he had dictated, I could not help saying enthusiastically how much this particular account (dealing with Marlowe) had moved me. Still burning with exuberance, I added admiringly that no one would ever pen so masterly a portrait again; hereupon, turning abruptly away, he bit his lip, threw the sheets of paper down and growled scornfully: "Don't talk such nonsense! Masterly? What would you know about it?" This brusque remark (probably just a shield hastily assumed to hide his impatient modesty) was enough to ruin my day. And in the afternoon, when I was alone with his wife, I suddenly fell into a kind of fit of hysteria, grasped her hands and said: "Tell me, why does he hate me so? Why does he despise me so much? What have I done to him, why does everything I say irritate him? Help me—tell me what to do! Why can't he bear me—tell me, please tell me!"

At this, assailed by my wild outburst, she turned a bright eye on me. "Not bear you?" And a laugh broke from her mouth, a laugh rising to such shrill heights of malice that I involuntarily flinched. "Not bear you?" she repeated, looking angrily into my startled eyes. But then she bent closer—her gaze gradually softened and then became even softer, almost sympathetic—and suddenly, for the first time, she stroked my hair. "Oh, you really are a child, a stupid child who notices nothing, sees nothing, knows nothing. But it's better that way— or you would be even more confused."

And with a sudden movement she turned away.

I SOUGHT CALM in vain—as if tied up in a black sack in an anxious dream from which there was no awakening, I struggled to understand, to rouse myself from the mysterious confusion of these conflicting feelings.

Four months had passed in this way—weeks of self-improvement and transformation such as I had never imagined. The term was fast approaching an end, and I faced the imminent vacation with a sense of dread, for I loved my purgatory, and the soberly non-intellectual atmosphere of my home threatened me like exile and deprivation. I was already hatching secret plans to pretend to my parents that important work kept me here, weaving a skilful tissue of lies and excuses to prolong my present existence, although it was devouring me. But the day and the hour had long ago been ordained for me elsewhere. That hour hung invisibly over me, just as the sound of the bell striking midday lies latent in the metal, ready to chime suddenly and gravely, urging laggards to work or to departure.

How well that fateful evening began, how deceptively well! I had been sitting at table with the two of them—the windows were open, and a twilit sky with white clouds was slowly filling their darkened frames: there was something mild and clear in their majestically hovering glow; one could not help feeling it deep within. His wife and I had been talking more casually, more easily, with more animation than usual. My teacher sat in silence, ignoring our conversation, but his silence presided over it with folded wings, so to speak. Looking sideways, I glanced surreptitiously at him—there was something curiously radiant about him today, a restlessness devoid of anything nervous, like the movement of those summer clouds. Sometimes he took his wine glass and held it up to the light to appreciate the colour, and when my happy glance followed that gesture he smiled slightly and raised the glass to me. I had seldom seen his face so untroubled, his movements so smooth and composed; he sat there in almost solemn cheerfulness, as if he heard music in the street outside, or were listening to some unseen conversation. His lips, around which tiny movements usually played, were still and soft as a peeled fruit, and his forehead when he turned it gently to the window took on the refraction of the mild light and seemed to me nobler than ever. It was wonderful to see him at peace like that: I did not know whether it was the reflection of the pure summer evening, whether the mild, soft air did him good, or whether some pleasant thought were illuminating him from within. But used as I was to reading his countenance like a book, I felt that today a kinder God had smoothed out the folds and crevices of his heart.

And it was with curious solemnity, too, that he rose and with his usual movement of the head invited me to follow him to his study: for a man who normally moved fast, he trod with strange gravity. Then he turned back, took an unopened bottle of wine from the sideboard— this too was unusual—and carried it thoughtfully into the study with him. His wife, like me, seemed to notice something strange in his behaviour; she looked up from her needlework with surprise in her eyes and, silent and intent, observed his unusually measured step as we went to the study to work.

The familiar dimness of the darkened room awaited us as usual; there was only a golden circle of light cast by the lamp on the piled white sheets of paper lying ready. I sat in my usual place and repeated the last few sentences of the manuscript; he always needed to hear the rhythm, which acted as a tuning fork, to get himself in the right mood and let the words stream on. But while he usually started immediately once that rhythm was established, this time no words came. Silence spread in the room, a tense silence already pressing in on us from the walls. He still seemed not quite to have collected himself, for I heard him pacing nervously behind my back. "Read it over again!" Odd how restlessly his voice suddenly vibrated. I repeated the last few paragraphs: now he started, going straight on from what I had said, dictating more abruptly but faster and with more consistency than usual. Five sentences set the scene; until now he had been describing the cultural prerequisites of the drama, painting a fresco of the period, an outline of its history. Now he turned to the drama itself, a genre finally settling down after all its vagabond wanderings, its rides across country in carts, building itself a home licensed by right and privilege, first the Rose Theatre and the Fortuna, wooden houses for plays that were wooden themselves, but then the workmen build a new wooden structure to match the broader breast of the new poetic genre, grown to virility; it rises on the banks of the Thames, on piles thrust into the damp and otherwise unprofitable muddy ground, a massive wooden building with an ungainly hexagonal tower, the Globe Theatre, where Shakespeare, the great master, will strut the stage. As if cast up by the sea like a strange ship, with a piratical red flag on the topmost mast, it stands there firmly anchored in the mud. The groundlings push and shove noisily on the floor of the theatre, as if in harbour, the finer folk smile down and chat idly with the players. Impatiently, they call for the play to begin. They stamp and shout, bang the hilts of their daggers on the boards, until at last a few flickering candles are brought out to illuminate the stage below, and casually costumed figures step forward to perform what appears to be an improvised comedy.

And then—I remember his words to this day—"a storm of words suddenly blows up, the sea, the endless sea of passion, sends its bloody waves surging out from these wooden walls to reach all times, all parts of the human heart, inexhaustible, unfathomable, merry and tragic, full of diversity, a unique image of mankind—the theatre of England, the drama of Shakespeare."

With these words, uttered in an elevated tone, he suddenly ceased. A long, heavy silence followed. Alarmed, I turned round: my teacher, one hand clutching the table, stood there with the look of exhaustion I knew well. But this time there was something alarming in his rigidity. I jumped up, fearing that something had happened to him, and asked anxiously whether I should stop. He just looked at me, breathless, his gaze fixed, and remained there immobile for a while. But then his starry eye shone bright blue again, his lips relaxed, he stepped towards me. "Well—haven't you noticed anything?" He looked hard at me. "Noticed what?" I stammered uncertainly. Then he took a deep breath and smiled slightly; after long months, I felt that enveloping, soft and tender gaze again. "The first part is finished." I had difficulty in suppressing a cry of joy, so warmly did my surprise surge through me. How could I have missed seeing it? Yes, there was the whole structure, magnificently built on foundations of the distant past, now on the threshold of its grand design:

now they could enter, Marlowe, Ben Jonson, Shakespeare, striding the stage victorious. The great work was celebrating its first anniversary. I made haste to count the pages. This first part amounted to a hundred and seventy close-written sheets, and was the most difficult, for what came next could be freely drawn, while hitherto the account had been closely bound to the historical facts. There was no doubt of it, he would complete his work—our work!

Did I shout aloud, did I dance around with joy, with pride, with delight? I don't know. But my enthusiasm must have taken unforeseen forms of exuberance, since his smiling gaze moved to me as I quickly read over the last few words, eagerly counted the pages, put them together, weighed them in my hand, felt them lovingly, and already, with my calculations running on ahead, I was imagining what it might be like when we had finished the whole book. He saw his own hidden pride, deeply concealed and dammed up as it was, reflected in my joy; touched, he looked at me with a smile. Then he slowly came very, very close to me, put out both hands and took mine; unmovingly, he looked at me. Gradually his pupils, which usually held only a quivering and sporadic play of colour, filled with that clear and radiant blue which, of all the elements, only the depths of water and of human feeling can represent. And this brilliant blue shone from his eyes, blazed out, penetrating me; I felt its surge of warmth moving softly to my inmost being, spreading there, extending into a sense of strange delight; my whole breast suddenly broadened with that vaulting, swelling power, and I felt an Italian noonday sun rising within me. "I know," said his voice, echoing above this brilliance, "that I would never have begun this work without you. I shall never forget what you have done. You gave my tired mind the spur it needed, and what remains of my lost, wasted life you and you alone have salvaged! No one has ever done more for me, no one has helped me so faithfully. And so it is you," he concluded, changing from the formal *Sie* to the familiar *du* pronoun—"it is you whom I must thank. Come! Let us sit together like brothers for a while!"

He drew me gently to the table and picked up the bottle standing ready. There were two glasses there as well—he had intended this symbolic sharing of the wine as a visible sign of his gratitude to me. I was trembling with joy, for nothing more violently confuses one's inner sense than the sudden granting of an ardent wish. The sign of his confidence, the open sign for which I had unconsciously been longing, had found the best possible means of expression in his thanks: the fraternal use of *du*, offered despite the gulf of years between us, was made seven times more precious by the obstacle that gulf represented. The bottle was about to strike its note, the still silent celebratory bottle which would soothe my anxieties for ever, replacing them with faith, and already my inner mind was ringing out as clearly as that quivering, bright note—when one small obstacle halted the festive moment: the bottle was still corked, and we had no corkscrew. He was about to go and fetch one, but guessing his intention I ran impatiently ahead of him to the dining-room—for I burned to experience that moment, the final pacification of my heart, the public statement of his regard for me.

As I ran impetuously through the doorway into the lighted corridor, I collided in the dark with something soft which hastily gave way—it was my teacher's wife, who had obviously been listening at the door. But strange to say, violently as I had collided with her she uttered not a sound, only stepped back in silence, and I myself, incapable of any movement, was so surprised that I said nothing either. This lasted for a moment—we both stood there in silence, feeling ashamed, she caught eavesdropping, I frozen to the spot by this unexpected discovery. But then there was a quiet footstep in the dark, a light came on, and I saw her, pale and defiant, standing with her back to the cupboard; her gaze studied me gravely, and there was something dark, admonitory and threatening in her immobile bearing. However, she said not a word.

My hands were shaking when, after groping around nervously for some time, half-blinded, I finally found the corkscrew; I had to pass her twice, and when I looked up I met that fixed gaze, gleaming hard and dark as polished wood. Nothing about her betrayed any shame at having been found secretly eavesdropping; on the contrary, her eyes, sharp and determined, were now darting threats which I could not understand, and her defiant attitude showed that she was not minded to move from this unseemly position, but intended to go on keeping watch and listening. Her superior strength of will confused me; unconsciously, I avoided the steady glance bent on me like a warning. And when finally, with uncertain step, I crept back into the room where my teacher was impatiently holding the bottle, the boundless joy I had just felt had frozen into a strange anxiety.

But how unconcernedly he was waiting, how cheerfully his gaze moved to me—I had always dreamed of seeing him like that some day, with the cloud of melancholy removed from his brow! Yet now that it was at peace for the first time, ardently turned to me, every word failed me; all my secret joy seeped away as if through hidden pores. Confused, indeed ashamed, I heard him thanking me again, still using the familiar *du*, and our glasses touched with a silvery sound. Putting his arm around me in friendly fashion, he led me over to the armchairs, where we sat opposite each other, his hand placed loosely in mine; for the first time I felt that he was entirely open and at ease. But words failed me; my glance involuntarily kept going to the door, where I feared she might still be standing and listening. She can hear us, I kept thinking, she can hear every word he says to me, every word I say to him—why today, why today of all days? And when, with that warm gaze enveloping me, he suddenly said: "There's something I would like to tell you about my own youth today," I put out a hand to stop him, showing such alarm that he looked up in surprise. "Not today," I stammered, "not today … please forgive me." The idea of his giving himself away to an eavesdropper whose presence I must conceal from him was too terrible.

Uncertainly, my teacher looked at me. "What's the matter?" he asked, sounding slightly displeased.

"I'm tired … forgive me … somehow it's been too much for me … I think," and here I rose to my feet, trembling, "I think I'd better go." Involuntarily my glance went past him to the door, where I could not help feeling that hostile curiosity must still be jealously on watch behind the wood.

Moving slowly, he too rose from his chair. A shadow moved over his suddenly tired face. "Are you really going already … today, of all days?" He held my hand; imperceptible pressure made it heavy. But suddenly he dropped it abruptly, like a stone. "A pity," he said, disappointed, "I was so much looking forward to speaking freely to you for once. A pity!" For a moment a profound sigh hovered like a dark butterfly in the room. I was deeply ashamed, and I felt a curiously inexplicable fear; uncertainly, I stepped back and closed the door of the room behind me.

I GROPED MY WAY laboriously up to my room and threw myself on the bed. But I could not sleep. Never before had I felt so strongly that my living quarters were separated from theirs only by thin floorboards, that there was only the impermeable dark wood between us. And now, with my sharpened senses and as if by magic, I sensed them both awake below me. Without seeing or hearing, I saw and heard him pacing restlessly up and down his study, while she sat silently or wandered around listening elsewhere. But I felt that both of them had their eyes open, and their wakefulness was horribly imparted to me—it was a nightmare, the whole heavy, silent house with its shadows and darkness suddenly weighing down on me.

I threw the covers off. My hands were sweating. What place had I reached? I had sensed the secret quite close, its hot breath already on my face, and now it had retreated again, but its shadow, its silent, opaque shadow still murmured in the air, I felt it as a dangerous presence in the house, stalking on quiet paws like a cat, always there, leaping back and forth, always touching and confusing me with its electrically charged fur, warm yet ghostly. And in the dark I kept feeling his encompassing gaze, soft as his proffered hand, and that other glance, the keen, threatening, alarmed look in his wife's eyes. What business did I have in their secret, why did the pair of them bring me into the midst of their passion with my eyes blindfolded, why were they chasing me into the preserves of their own unintelligible strife, each forcing a blazing accumulation of anger and hatred into my mind?

My brow was still burning. I sat up and opened the window. Outside, the town lay peaceful under the summer clouds; windows were still lamplit, but the people sitting in them were united by calm conversation, cheered by a book or by domestic music-making. And surely calm sleep reigned where darkness already showed behind the white window frames. Above all these resting rooftops, mild peace hovered like the moon in silvery mists, a relaxed and gentle silence, and the eleven strokes of the clock striking from the tower fell lightly on all their ears, whether they chanced to be listening or were dreaming. Only I still felt wide awake, balefully beset by strange thoughts. Some inner sense was feverishly trying to make out that confused murmuring.

Suddenly I started. Wasn't that a footstep on the stairs? I sat up, listening. Sure enough, something was making its way blindly up them, something in the nature of cautious, hesitant, uncertain footsteps—I knew the creak and groan of the worn wood. Those footsteps could only be coming towards me, only to me, since no one else lived up here on the top floor except for the deaf old lady, and she would have been asleep long ago and never had visitors. Was it my teacher? No, that was not his rapid, restless tread; these footsteps hesitated and waited cravenly—there it was again!—on every step: an intruder, a criminal might approach like this, not a friend. I strained my ears so intently that there was a roaring in them. And suddenly a frosty sensation crept up my bare legs.

Then the latch clicked quietly—my sinister visitor must already be on the threshold. A faint draught of air on my bare toes told me that the outer door had been opened, yet no one else, apart from my teacher, had the key. But if it were he—why so hesitant, so strange? Was he anxious about me, did he want to see if I was all right? And why did my sinister visitor hesitate now, just outside the door? For his furtively creeping step had suddenly stopped. I was equally immobile as I faced the horror. I felt as if I ought to scream, but my throat was closed with mucus. I wanted to open the door; my feet refused to move. Only a thin partition now divided me and my mysterious visitor, but neither of us took a step forward to face the other.

Then the bell in the tower struck—only once, a quarter-to-twelve. But it broke the spell. I flung the door open.

And indeed there stood my teacher, candle in hand. The draught from the door as it suddenly swung open made the flame leap with a blue light, and behind it, gigantic and separated from him as he stood there motionless, his quivering shadow flickered drunkenly over the wall behind him. But he too moved when he saw me; he pulled himself together like a man woken from sleep by a sudden breath of keen air, shivering and involuntarily pulling the covers around him. Only then did he step back, the dripping candle swaying in his hand.

I trembled, scared to death. "What's the matter?" was all I could stammer. He looked at me without speaking; words failed him too. At last he put the candle down on the chest of drawers, and immediately the bat-like fluttering of shadows around the room was calmed. Finally he stammered: "I wanted … I wanted … "

Again his voice failed. He stood looking at the floor like a thief caught in the act. This anxiety was unbearable as we stood there, I in my nightshirt, trembling with cold, he with his back bowed, confused with shame.

Suddenly the frail figure moved. He came towards me—at first a smile, malevolent, faun-like, a dangerous, glinting smile that showed only in his eyes (for his lips were compressed) grinned rigidly at me for a moment like a strange mask—and then the voice spoke, sharp as a snake's forked tongue: "I only wanted to say … we'd better not. You … It isn't right, not a young student and his teacher, do you understand?" He had changed back to the formal *Sie* pronoun. "One must keep one's distance … distance … distance … "

And he looked at me with such hatred, such insulting and vehement ill-will that his hand involuntarily clenched. I stumbled back. Was he mad? Was he drunk? There he stood, fist clenched, as if he were about to fling himself on me or strike me in the face.

But the horror lasted only a second; and then that penetrating glance was lowered and turned in on itself. He turned, muttered something that sounded like an apology, and picked up the candle. His shadow, an obedient black devil which had fallen to the floor, rose again and swirled to the door ahead of him. And then he himself was gone, before I had summoned up the strength to think of anything to say. The latch of the door clicked shut; the stairs creaked heavily, painfully, under what seemed his hasty footsteps.

I SHALL NOT FORGET that night; cold rage alternated wildly with a baffled, incandescent despair. Thoughts flashed through my mind like flaring rockets. Why does he torment me, my anguished and tortured mind asked a hundred times, why does he hate me so much that he will creep upstairs at night on purpose to hurl such hostile insults in my face? What have I done to him, what was I supposed to do instead? How am I to make my peace without knowing what I've done to hurt him? I flung myself on the bed in a fever, got up, buried myself under the covers again, but that ghostly picture was always in my mind's eye: my teacher slinking up here, confused by my presence, and behind him, mysterious and strange, that monstrous shadow tumbling over the wall.

When I woke in the morning, after a short period of brief and shallow slumber, I told myself at first that I must have been dreaming. But there were still round, yellow, congealed drops of candle wax on the chest of drawers. And in the middle of the bright, sunlit room my dreadful memory of last night's furtive visitor returned again and again.

I stayed in my room all morning. The thought of meeting him sapped my strength. I tried to write, to read;

nothing was any use. My nerves were undermined and might fall into shattering convulsions at any moment, I might begin sobbing and howling—for I could see my own fingers trembling like leaves on a strange tree, I was unable to still them, and my knees felt as weak as if the sinews had been cut. What was I to do? What was I to do? I asked myself that question over and over again until I was exhausted; the blood was already pounding in my temples, there were blue shadows under my eyes. But I could not go out, could not go downstairs, could not suddenly face him without being certain of myself, without having some strength in my nerves again. Once again I flung myself on the bed, hungry, confused, unwashed, distressed, and once again my senses tried to penetrate the thin floorboards: where was he now, what was he doing, was he awake like me, was he as desperate as I myself?

Midday came, and I still lay on the fiery rack of my confusion, when I heard a step on the stairs at last. All my nerves jangled with alarm, but it was a light, care-free step running upstairs two at a time—and now a hand was knocking at the door. I jumped up without opening it. "Who's there?" I asked. "Why don't you come downstairs to eat?" replied his wife's voice, in some annoyance. "Aren't you well?" "No, no," I stammered in confusion. "Just coming, just coming." And now there was nothing I could do but get my clothes on and go downstairs. But my limbs were so unsteady that I had to cling to the banister.

I went into the dining-room. My teacher's wife was waiting in front of one of the two places that had been laid, and greeted me with a mild reproach for having to be reminded. His own place was empty. I felt the blood rise to my face. What did his unexpected absence mean? Did he fear our meeting even more than I did? Was he ashamed, or didn't he want to share a table with me any more? Finally I made up my mind to ask whether the Professor wasn't coming in to lunch.

She looked up in surprise. "Don't you know he went away this morning, then?" "Went away?" I stammered. "Where to?" Her face immediately tensed. "My husband did not see fit to tell me, but probably— well another of his usual excursions." Then she turned towards me with a sudden sharp, questioning look. "You mean that you don't know? He went up to see you on purpose last night—I thought it was to say goodbye … how strange, how very strange that he didn't tell you either."

"Me!" I could utter only a scream. And to my shame and disgrace, that scream swept away everything that had been so dangerously dammed up in me during the last few hours. Suddenly it all burst out in a sobbing, howling, raging convulsion—I vomited a gurgling torrent of words and screams tumbling over one another,

a great swirling mass of confused desperation, I wept—
no, I shook, my trembling mouth brought up all the torment that had accumulated inside me. Fists drumming
frantically on the table like a child throwing a tantrum,
face covered with tears, I let out what had been hanging over me for weeks like a thunderstorm. And while I
found relief in that wild outbreak, I also felt boundless
shame in giving so much of myself away to her.

"What on earth is the matter? For God's sake!" She
had risen to her feet, astonished. But then she hurried
up to me and led me from the table to the sofa. "Lie here
and calm down." She stroked my hands, she passed
her own hands over my hair, while the aftermath of
my spasms still shook my trembling body. "Don't distress yourself, Roland—please don't distress yourself. I
know all about it, I could feel it coming." She was still
stroking my hair, but suddenly her voice grew hard. "I
know just how he can confuse one, nobody knows better. But please believe me, I always wanted to warn you
when I saw you leaning on him so much, on a man who
can't even support himself. You don't know him, you're
blind. You are a child—you don't know anything, or
not yet, not today. Or perhaps today you have begun to
understand something for the first time—in which case
all the better for him and for you."

She remained bending over me in warm concern,
and as if from vitreous depths I felt her words and the

110

soothing touch of calming hands. It did me good to feel
a breath of sympathy again at long, long last, and then
to sense a woman's tender, almost maternal hand so
close once more. Perhaps I had gone without that too
long as well, and now that I felt, through the veils of my
distress, a tenderly concerned woman's sympathy, some
comfort came over me in the midst of my pain. But oh,
how ashamed I was, how ashamed of that treacherous
fit in which I had let out my despair! And it was against
my will that, sitting up with difficulty, I brought it all out
again in a rushing, stammering flood of words, all he
had done to me—how he had rejected and persecuted
me, then shown me kindness again, how he was harsh
to me for no reason, no cause—a torturer, but one to
whom ties of affection bound me, whom I hated even
as I loved him and loved even as I hated him. Once
more I began to work myself up to such a pitch that
she had to soothe me again. Once more soft hands
gently pressed me back on the ottoman from which I
had jumped up in my agitation. At last I calmed down.
She preserved a curiously thoughtful silence; I felt that
she understood everything, perhaps even more than I
did myself.

For a few minutes this silence linked us. Then she stood
up. "There—now you've been a child long enough; you
must be a man again. Sit down at the table and have
something to eat. Nothing tragic has happened—it

was just a misunderstanding that will soon be cleared up." And when I made some kind of protest, she added firmly, "It will soon be cleared up, because I'm not letting him play with you and confuse you like that any more. There must be an end to all this; he must finally learn to control himself. You're too good for his dangerous games. I shall speak to him, trust me. But now come and have something to eat."

Ashamed and without any volition of my own, I let her lead me back to the table. She talked of unimportant matters with a certain rapid eagerness, and I was inwardly grateful to her for seeming to ignore my wild outburst and forgetting it again. Tomorrow, she said, was Sunday, and she was going for an outing on a nearby lake with a lecturer called W and his fiancée, I ought to come too, cheer myself up, take a rest from my books. All the malaise I felt, she said, just showed that I was overworking and my nerves were overstretched; once I was in the water swimming, or out on a walk, my body would soon regain its equilibrium.

I said I would go. Anything but solitude now, anything but my room, anything but my thoughts circling in the dark. "And don't stay in this afternoon either! Go for a stroll, take some exercise, amuse yourself!" she urged me. Strange, I thought, how she guesses at my most intimate feelings, how even though she's a stranger to me she knows what I need and what hurts me, while I, who ought to know, fail to see it and torment myself. I told her I would do as she suggested. And looking up gratefully, I saw a new expression on her face: the mocking, lively face that sometimes gave her the look of a pert, easy-going boy had softened to a sympathetic gaze; I had never seen her so grave before. Why does he never look at me so kindly, asked something confused and yearning in me, why does he never seem to know when he is hurting me? Why has he never laid such helpful, tender hands on my hair, on my own hands? And gratefully I kissed hers, which she abruptly, almost violently withdrew. "Don't torment yourself," she repeated, and her voice seemed close to me.

But then her lips pressed together in a hard line again, and suddenly straightening her back she said, quietly: "Believe me, he doesn't deserve it."

And that almost inaudibly whispered remark struck pain into my almost pacified heart once more.

WHAT I SET OUT TO DO that afternoon and evening seems so ridiculous and childish that for years I have blushed to think of it—indeed, internal censorship was quick to blot out its memory. Well, today I am no longer ashamed of my clumsy foolishness—on the contrary, how well do I understand the impulsive, muddled ideas of the passionate youth who wanted to vault over his own confused feelings by main force.

I see myself as if at the end of a hugely long corridor, viewed through a telescope: the desperate, desolate boy climbing up to his room, not knowing what to do with himself. And then putting on another coat, bracing himself to adopt a different gait, making wild and determined gestures, and suddenly marching out into the street with a vigorously energetic tread. Yes, there I go, I recognize myself, I know every thought in the head of the poor silly, tormented boy I was then; suddenly, in front of the mirror in fact, I pulled myself together and said: "Who cares for him! To hell with him! Why should I torment myself over that old fool! She's right—I ought to have some fun, I ought to amuse myself for once! Here goes!"

And that, indeed, was how I walked out into the street. At first it was an effort to liberate myself—then a race, a mere cowardly flight from the realization that my cheerful fun wasn't so cheerful after all, and that block of ice still weighed as heavily on my heart as before. I still remember how I walked along, my heavy stick clasped firmly in my hand, looking keenly at every student, with a dangerous desire to pick a quarrel with someone raging in me, a wish to take out my anger, which had no outlet, on the first man I came across. But fortunately no one troubled to pay me any attention. So I made my way to the café usually frequented by my fellow students at the university, ready to sit down at their table unasked and take the slightest gibe as provocation. Once again, however, my readiness to quarrel found no object—the fine day had tempted most of them to go out of town, and the two or three sitting together greeted me civilly and gave my fevered, touchy mood not the slightest excuse to take offence. I soon rose from the table, feeling irritated, and went off to what is now no longer a dubious inn in the suburbs, where the riff-raff of the town, out for a good time, crowded close together among beer fumes and smoke to the loud music of a ladies' wind band. I tipped two or three glasses of liquor hastily down my throat, invited a lady of easy virtue to my table along with her friend, also a hard-bitten and much painted demi-mondaine, and took a perverted pleasure in drawing attention to myself. Everyone in the little town knew me, everyone knew I was the Professor's student, and as for the women, their bold dress and conduct made it obvious what they were—so I relished the false, silly pleasure of compromising my reputation and with it (so I foolishly thought) his too; let them all see that I don't care for him, I thought, let them see I don't mind what he thinks—and I paid court to my bosomy female companion in front of everyone in the most shameless and unseemly manner. I was intoxicated by my angry ill-will, and we were soon literally intoxicated too, for we drank everything indiscriminately—wine, spirits, beer—and carried on so boisterously that chairs toppled over and our neighbours prudently moved away. But I was not ashamed, on the contrary; let him hear about this, I raged foolishly, let him see how little I care for him, I'm not upset, I don't feel injured, far from it: "Wine, more wine!" I shouted, banging my fist down on the table so that the glasses shook. Finally I left with the two women, one on my right arm, the other on my left, marching straight down the high street where the usual nine o'clock promenade brought students and their girls, citizens and military men together for a pleasant stroll—like a soiled and unsteady clover leaf, the three of us rampaged along the road making so much noise that in the end a policeman, looking annoyed, approached us and firmly told us to pipe down. I cannot describe what happened next in detail—a blue haze of strong liquor blurs my memory, I know only that, disgusted by the two intoxicated women and scarcely in control of my senses any more, I bought myself free of them, drank more coffee and cognac somewhere, and then, outside the university building, delivered myself of a tirade against all professors, for the delectation of the young fellows who gathered around me. Then, out of a vague wish to soil myself yet further and do him an injury—oh, the delusions of passionate and confused anger!—I meant to go into a house of ill repute, but I couldn't find the way, and finally staggered sullenly home. My unsteady hand had some trouble in opening the front door of the building, and it was with difficulty that I dragged myself up the first few steps of the stairs.

But then, outside his door, all my oppressive sense of intoxication vanished as if my head had suddenly been doused in icy water. Instantly sobered, I was staring into the distorted face of my own helplessly raging foolishness. I cringed with shame. And very quietly, grovelling like a beaten dog, hoping that no one would hear me, I slunk up to my room.

I SLEPT LIKE THE DEAD; when I woke, sunlight was flooding the floor and rising slowly to the edge of my bed. I got out of it with a sudden movement. Memories of the previous evening gradually came into my aching head, but I repressed the shame, I wasn't going to feel ashamed any more. It was his fault, after all, I insisted to myself, it was all his fault that I'd been so dissolute. I calmed myself by thinking that yesterday's events were nothing but a normal student prank, perfectly permissible in a man who had done nothing but work and work for weeks on end; but I did not feel happy with my own self-justification, and rather apprehensively I timidly went down to my teacher's wife, remembering that I had agreed yesterday to go on her outing with her.

It was odd—no sooner did I touch the handle of his door than he was present in me again, but so too was that burning, unreasonable, churning pain, that raging despair. I knocked softly, and his wife came to let me in with a strangely soft expression. "What nonsense have you been up to, Roland?" she said, but sympathetically rather than reproachfully. "Why do you give yourself such a bad time?" I was taken aback: so she had already heard of my foolish conduct. But she immediately

119

helped me to get over my embarrassment. "We're going to be sensible today, though. Dr W and his fiancée will be here at ten, and then we'll go out to the lake and row and swim and forget all that stupid stuff." With great trepidation I ventured to ask, unnecessarily, whether the Professor was back yet. She looked at me without answering, and I knew for myself that it was a pointless question.

At ten sharp the lecturer arrived, a young physicist who, rather isolated himself as a Jew among the other academics, was really the only one of them who mixed with our reclusive little society; he was accompanied by his fiancée, or more likely his mistress, a young girl who was always laughing artlessly in a slightly silly way, but that made her just the right company for such an improvised excursion. First we travelled by train—eating, talking and laughing all the way—to a tiny lake nearby, and after my weeks of strenuous gravity I was so unused to any light-hearted conversation that even this one hour of it went to my head like slightly sparkling wine. Their childish high spirits succeeded entirely in diverting my thoughts from the subject that they usually circled, like bees buzzing around a darkly oozing honeycomb, and no sooner did I step into the open air and feel my muscles stretched to the full again in an improvised race with the young woman than I was the fit, carefree boy of the past once more.

Down at the lake we hired two rowing boats; my teacher's wife steered mine, and the lecturer and his girlfriend shared the rowing between them in the other. No sooner had we pushed off than a spirit of competitive sport made us try to overtake each other. I was at a clear disadvantage, since there were two people rowing the other boat and I had to contend with them on my own, but throwing off my coat I plied the oars so vigorously, being a trained oarsman myself, that my strong strokes kept drawing us ahead. We spurred ourselves on with mocking remarks called from boat to boat, and careless of the burning July sun, indifferent to the sweat inelegantly drenching us, we laboured to outstrip one another, irrepressible galley slaves labouring in the heat of athletic pleasure. At last our goal was near, a little tree-grown tongue of land projecting into the lake, we rowed harder than ever, and to the triumph of my companion in the boat, herself in the grip of the spirit of competition, our keel was the first to ground on the beach. I climbed out, hot, perspiring, intoxicated by the unfamiliar sun, the roar of my excited blood in my veins and by the pleasure of victory—my heart was hammering away and my sweaty clothes clung close to my body. The lecturer was in no better state, and instead of earning praise for our determination in the struggle we were the object of much high-spirited mockery from the women for our breathlessness and rather pitiful appearance. At last they allowed us a respite to cool off; amidst jokes and laughter, a ladies' changing room and a gentlemen's changing room were improvised to the right and left of a bush. We quickly put our swimming costumes on; pale underclothes and naked arms flashed into view on the other side of the bush, and the two women were already splashing happily in the water as we men got ready too. The lecturer, less exhausted than I was myself after defeating the two of them, immediately jumped in after the ladies, but as I had rowed a little too hard and could still feel my heart thudding against my ribs I lay comfortably in the shade for a while first, enjoying the sensation of the clouds moving over me and the pleasantly sweet droning sensation of weariness surging through the circulation of my blood.

But after a few minutes I heard loud shouts from the water: "Come on, Roland! We're having a swimming race! A swimming competition! A diving competition!" I stayed put; I felt as if I could lie like this for a thousand years, my skin gently warmed as the sun fell on it and at the same time cooled by the tenderly caressing breeze. But again I heard laughter, and the lecturer's voice: "He's on strike! We've really worn him out! You go and fetch the lazy fellow." And sure enough, I could hear someone splashing towards me, and then, from very close, her voice: "Come on, Roland! It's a swimming race! Let's show those two!" I didn't answer, I enjoyed making her look for me. "Where are you, then?" The gravel crunched, I heard bare feet running along the beach in search of me, and suddenly there she was, her wet swimming costume clinging to her boyishly slender body. "Oh, there you are, you lazy thing! Come along, lazybones, the others have almost reached the island." But I lay at ease on my back, stretching idly. "It's much nicer here. I'll follow later."

"He won't come in," she laughed, calling through her cupped hand in the direction of the water. "Then push the show-off in!" shouted the lecturer's voice back from afar. "Oh, do come on," she urged me impatiently, "don't let me down!" But I just yawned lazily. Then, in mingled jest and annoyance, she broke a twig off the bush as a switch. "Come on!" she repeated energetically, striking me a playful blow on the arm to encourage me. I started—she had hit too hard, and a thin red mark like blood ran over my arm. "Well, I'm certainly not coming now," I said, both joking and slightly angry myself. But at this, sounding really cross, she commanded: "Come on, will you! This minute!" And when, defiantly, I did not move, she struck another blow, harder this time, a sharp and burning stroke. All at once I jumped up angrily to snatch the switch away from her, she retreated, but I seized her arm. Involuntarily, as we wrestled for possession of the switch, our half-naked bodies came close.

And when I seized her arm and twisted the wrist to make her drop it, and she bent far back trying to evade me, there was a sudden snapping sound—the buckle holding the shoulder strap of her swimming costume had come apart, the left cup fell from her bare breast, and its erect red nipple met my eye. I could not help looking, just for a second, but I was cast into a state of confusion—trembling and ashamed, I let go of the hand I had been clutching. She turned away, blushing, to perform a makeshift repair on the broken buckle with a hairpin. I stood there at a loss for words. She was silent too. And from that moment on there was an awkward, suppressed uneasiness between the two of us.

"HALLO … hallo … where are you both?" the voices came echoing over from the little island. "Just coming," I replied quickly, and glad to escape more embarrassment I threw myself vigorously into the water. A couple of diving strokes, the inspiring pleasure of driving myself forward through the water, the clarity and cold of the unfeeling element, and already that dangerous murmuring and hissing in my blood receded, as if washed away by a stronger, purer pleasure. I soon caught up with the other two, challenged the lecturer, who was not a very strong athlete, to a series of competitions in which I emerged the victor, and then we swam back to the little tongue of land where my teacher's wife, who had stayed behind and was already dressed again, was waiting to organize a cheerful picnic unpacked from the baskets we had brought along. But exuberant as the light-hearted conversation was between the four of us, we two involuntarily avoided speaking to each other directly—we talked and laughed as if ignoring one another. And when our glances did meet we hastily looked away again, in an unspoken complicity of feeling: the embarrassment of the little incident had not yet ebbed away, and each of us sensed, ashamed and uneasy, that the other was remembering it too.

The rest of the afternoon passed quickly, with more rowing on the lake, but the heat of our enthusiasm for sport increasingly gave way to a pleasant weariness: the wine, the warmth, the sun we had soaked up gradually seeped further into our blood, making it flow redder than before. The lecturer and his girlfriend were already allowing themselves little familiarities which the two of us were obliged to watch with a certain embarrassment; they moved closer and closer to each other while we kept our distance all the more scrupulously; but the fact that we were two couples was particularly evident when the pair of them lagged behind on the woodland path, obviously to kiss undisturbed, and when we two were left alone awkwardness inhibited our conversation. In the end all four of us were glad to be back in the train, the engaged couple looking forward to an evening together, we happy to escape an embarrassing situation.

The lecturer and his girlfriend accompanied us home. We all went upstairs together, and no soon were we inside than I once more felt the tormenting premonition of his presence, the presence for which I confusedly yearned. "Oh, if only he were back!" I thought impatiently. And just as if she had divined the sigh which did not quite rise from my lips, she said: "Let's see if he's back yet."

We went in. The place was quiet. Everything in his study was still abandoned; unconsciously, my agitated feelings imagined his oppressed, tragic figure in the empty chair. But the sheets of paper lay untouched, waiting as I was waiting myself. Then bitterness returned: why had he fled, why had he left me alone? Jealous rage rose more and more grimly within me, once again I dully felt my foolishly confused desire to do something to harm him, something hateful.

His wife had followed me. "You'll stay to supper, I hope? You ought not to be alone today." How did she know I was afraid of my empty room, of the creaking of the stairs, of brooding over my memories? She always did guess everything going on in me, every unspoken thought, every ignoble desire.

A kind of fear came over me, a fear of myself and the vague turmoil of hatred within me, and I wanted to refuse. But cravenly, I did not venture to say no.

I HAVE ALWAYS had a horror of adultery, but not for any self-righteous moral reasons, not out of prudery and convention, not so much because taking possession of a strange body is theft committed in the dark, but because almost every woman will give away her husband's most intimate secrets at such moments—every one of them is a Delilah stealing his most human secret from the man she is deceiving and casting it before a stranger, the secret of his strength or of his weakness. The betrayal, it seems to me, is not that a woman gives herself of her own free will but that then, to justify herself, she will uncover her husband's loins and expose him unknown to himself, as if in his sleep, to the curiosity of another man, and to scornfully relished laughter.

It is not, therefore, that when confused by blind and angry desperation I took refuge in his wife's first sympathetic and only then tender embrace—ah, how fatefully swift is the move from one feeling to the other—it is not what I still feel today was the worst thing I ever did in my life (for it happened in spite of ourselves, we both plunged unconsciously, unknowingly, into those burning depths), but the fact that among the tumbled pillows I let her tell me intimate details of him, that I allowed her, all on edge as she was herself, to give away the innermost secrets of her marriage. Why did I suffer her, without repelling her, to tell me that he had not touched her physically for years, and to indulge in dark hints: why did I not command her to keep silent over this most intimate core of his being? But I was so eager to know his secret myself, so anxious to feel that he had injured me, her, everyone, that I dizzily accepted her angry confession of his neglect of her—after all, it was so like the sense of rejection I had felt myself! And so it was that the two of us, out of a shared and confused hatred, performed an act that looked like love, but while our bodies sought each other and came together we were both thinking and speaking of him all the time, of nothing but him. Sometimes what she said hurt me, and I was ashamed to be involved with what I disliked. But my body no longer obeyed my will, and instead wildly sought its own pleasure. Shuddering, I kissed the lips which were betraying the person I most loved.

Next morning I crept up to my room, the bitter flavour of disgust and shame in my mouth. Now that the warmth of her body no longer troubled my senses I felt the glaring reality, the repulsive nature of my betrayal. I knew at once that I would never again be able to look him in the face, never again take his hand—I had robbed myself, not him, of what meant most to me.

There was only one solution now: flight. Feverishly I packed all my things, piled my books into a stack, paid my landlady—he must not find me again, I must disappear from his life, mysteriously and for no apparent reason, just as he had disappeared from mine.

But amidst all this activity my hand suddenly froze. I had heard the creaking of the wooden stairs, footsteps coming rapidly up the steps—his footsteps.

I must have turned white as a sheet, for as soon as he entered he reacted with horror. "What's the matter with you, my boy? Are you unwell?"

I retreated. I flinched away from him as he was about to come closer and offer me a helping hand.

"What on earth is the matter?" he asked in alarm. "Has something happened to you? Or ... or are you still angry with me?"

I clung convulsively to the window frame. I could not look at him. His sympathetic, warm voice tore something like a wound open in me—close to fainting, I felt it well up in me, hot, very hot, burning and consuming, a glowing flood of shame.

He too stood there in surprise and confusion. And suddenly, with his voice very faint, hesitant and low, he whispered an odd question: "Has ... has someone ... been telling you something about me?"

Without turning to him, I made a gesture of denial. But some anxious idea seemed to be uppermost in his mind, and he repeated doggedly: "Tell me—admit it … has anyone been telling you something about me? Anyone—I'm not asking who."

I denied it again. He stood there at a loss. But suddenly he seemed to have noticed that my bags were packed, my books stacked together, and saw that his arrival had just interrupted my preparations to leave. Agitated, he came up to me. "You mean to go away, Roland, I can see you do … tell me the truth."

Then I pulled myself together. "I must go away … forgive me, I can't talk about it … I'll write to you." My constricted throat could utter no more, and my heart thudded with every word.

He stood quite still. Then, suddenly, that familiar weariness of his came over him. "It may be better this way, Roland … yes, of course, it is … for you, for everyone. But before you leave I would like to talk to you once more. Come at seven, at our usual time, and we'll say goodbye man to man. No flight from ourselves, though, no letters … that would be childish and unworthy … and what I would like to tell you is not for pen and paper. You will come, won't you?"

I only nodded. My gaze still dared not move from the window. But I saw none of the brightness of the morning any more; a dense, dark veil had dropped between me and the world.

At seven I entered that beloved room for the last time: early dusk filtered dimly through the portières, the smooth stone of the marble statues scarcely gleamed from the back of the room, and the books slumbered, black behind the mother-of-pearl shimmer of the glass doors over the bookcase. Ah, secret place of my memories, where the word became magical to me and I knew the intoxication and enchantment of the intellect as nowhere else—I always see you as you were at that hour of farewell, and I still see the venerated figure slowly, slowly rising from his chair and approaching me, a shadowy form, only the curved brow gleaming like an alabaster lamp in the dim light, and the white hair of an old man waving above it like drifting smoke. Now a hand, raised with difficulty, was proffered and sought mine, now I saw the eyes turned gravely towards me, and felt my arm gently taken as he led me back to the place where he was sitting.

"Sit down, Roland, and let us talk frankly. We are men and must be honest. I won't press you—but would it not be better for this last hour to bring full clarity between us? So tell me, why do you want to leave? Are you angry with me for that thoughtless insult?"

I made a gesture of denial. How terrible to think that he, the man betrayed, the man deceived, was still trying to take the blame on himself!

"Have I done you some other injury, consciously or unconsciously? I know I am sometimes rather strange.

And I have irritated and tormented you against my own will. I have never thanked you enough for all your support—I know it, I know it, I have always known it, even in those moments when I hurt you. Is that the reason—tell me, Roland, for I would like us to part from one another with honesty."

Once again I shook my head: I could not speak. His voice had been firm; now it became a little unsteady.

"Or … let me ask you again … has anyone told you anything about me, anything that you think base … repulsive … anything that … that makes you despise me?"

"No! No, no!" The protest burst from me like a sob: did he think I could despise him? I despise him!

His voice now grew impatient. "Then what is it? What else can it be? Are you tired of the work? Or does something else make you want to go? A woman … is it a woman?"

I said nothing. And that silence was probably so different in nature that he felt in it the positive answer to his question. He leaned closer and whispered very softly, but without agitation, without any agitation or anger at all:

"Is it a woman? Is it … my wife?"

I was still silent, and he understood. A tremor ran through my body: now, now, now he would burst out, attack me, strike me, chastise me … and I almost wanted him to whip me, the thief, the deceiver, whip me like a mangy dog from his desecrated home. But strangely, he remained entirely still … and he sounded almost relieved when he murmured as if to himself: "I might have known it." He paced up and down the room a couple of times. Then he stopped in front of me and said, as it seemed to me, almost dismissively:

"And that … that is what you take so hard? Didn't she tell you that she is free to do as she likes, take what she likes, that I have no rights over her? No right to forbid her anything, nor the least desire to do so … And why, for whose sake, should she have controlled herself, and for you of all people … you are young, you are bright, beautiful … you were close to us, how could she not love you, such a beautiful young man, how could she help but love you? For I … " Suddenly his voice began to falter, and he leaned close, so close that I felt his breath. Again I sensed the warm embrace of his gaze, again I saw that strange light in his eyes, just as it had been before in those rare and strange moments between us. He came ever closer.

And then he whispered softly, his lips hardly moving: "For I love you too."

D ID I START? Did I show involuntary alarm? My body must have made some movement of surprise or evasion, for he flinched back like a man rejected. A shadow fell over his face. "Do you despise me now?" he asked very quietly. "Am I repulsive to you?"

Why could I find nothing to say? Why did I simply sit there in silence, unlovingly, embarrassed, numbed, instead of going to the man who loved me and disabusing him of his mistaken fear? But all the memories were in wild turmoil within me; as if a cipher had suddenly solved the coded language of those incomprehensible messages, I now understood it all with terrible clarity: his tender approaches and his brusque defensiveness—shattered, I understood that visit in the night and his grimly determined flight from the passion I so enthusiastically pressed on him. Yes, I had always felt the love in him, tender and timid, now surging out, now forcibly inhibited again, I had loved and enjoyed it in the radiance fleetingly falling on me—yet as the word love now came from his bearded mouth, a sensuously tender sound, horror both sweet and terrible entered my mind. And much as I burned in humility and in pity for him, confused, trembling, shattered boy that I was,

I could find nothing to say in answer to his unexpected revelation of his passion.

He sat there crushed, staring at my silence. "It seems to you so terrible, then, so terrible," he murmured. "You too … you will not forgive me either, you to whom I have kept my mouth so firmly closed that I almost choked—from whom I have hidden myself as from no one else … but it's better for you to know it now, and then it will no longer weigh on my mind. It was too much for me anyway … oh, far too much … an end is better, better than such silence and concealment."

How sadly he spoke, his voice full of tenderness and shame; the trembling note in it went to my heart. I was ashamed of myself for preserving so cold, so unfeelingly frosty a silence before this man who had given me more than anyone alive, and who now so pointlessly humbled himself before me. My soul burned to say something comforting to him, but my trembling lips would not obey me. And so I sat awkwardly there, wretchedly shifting in my chair until, almost angrily, he tried to cheer me. "Don't sit there like that, Roland, in such dreadful silence … pull yourself together. Is it really so terrible? Are you so ashamed of me? It's all over now, you see, I have told you everything … let us at least say goodbye properly as two men, two friends should."

But I still had no power over myself. He touched my arm. "Come, Roland, sit down beside me. I feel easier now that you know, now that there's honesty between us at last … At first I kept fearing you might guess how dear you are to me … then I hoped you would feel it for yourself, so that I would be spared this confession … but now it has happened, now I am free, and now I can speak to you as I have never spoken to another living soul. For you have been closer to me than anyone else in all these years, I have loved you as I loved no one before you … Like no one else, my child, you have awakened the last spark in me. So as we part you should also know more of me than anyone else does. In all our time together I have felt your silent questioning so clearly … you alone shall know my full story. Do you want me to tell it to you?"

He saw my assent in my glance, in my confused and shattered expression.

"Come close then … come close to me. I cannot say such things out loud." I leaned forward—devoutly, I can only say. But no sooner was I sitting opposite him waiting, listening, than he rose again. "No, this won't do … you mustn't look at me or … or I can't talk about it." And he put out his hand to turn off the light.

Darkness fell over us. I sensed him near me, knew it from his breathing which somewhere passed into the unseen heavily, almost stertorously. And suddenly a voice rose in the air between us and told me the whole story of his life.

S INCE THAT EVENING when the man I so venerated opened up like a shell that had been tightly closed and told me his story, since that evening forty years ago, everything our writers and poets present as extraordinary in books, everything shown on stage as tragic drama, has seemed to me trivial and unimportant. Is it through complacency, cowardice, or because they take too short a view that they speak of nothing but the superficial, brightly lit plane of life where the senses openly and lawfully have room to play, while below in the vaults, in the deep caves and sewers of the heart, the true dangerous beasts of passion roam, glowing with phosphorescent light, coupling unseen and tearing each other apart in every fantastic form of convolution? Does the breath of those beasts alarm them, the hot and tearing breath of demonic urges, the exhalations of the burning blood, do they fear to dirty their dainty hands on the ulcers of humanity, or does their gaze, used to a more muted light, not find its way down the slippery, dangerous steps that drip with decay? And yet to those who truly know, no lust is like the lust for the hidden, no horror so primevally forceful as that which quivers around danger, no suffering more sacred than that which cannot express itself for shame.

But here a man was disclosing himself to me exactly as he was, opening up his inmost thoughts, eager to bare his battered, poisoned, burnt and festering heart. A wild delight like that of a flagellant tormented itself in the confession he had kept back for so many years. Only a man who had been ashamed all his life, cowering and hiding, could launch with such intoxication and so overwhelmed into so pitiless a confession. He was tearing the life from his breast piecemeal, and in that hour the boy I then was looked down for the first time into the unimaginable depths of human emotion.

At first his voice hovered in the room as if disembodied, an indistinct haze of agitation, uncertainly hinting at secret events, yet this laborious control of passion in itself made me divine the force it was to show, just as when you hear certain markedly decelerating bars of music, foreshadowing a rapid rhythm, you feel the furioso in your nerves in advance. But then images began to flicker up, raised trembling by the inner storm of passion and gradually showing in the light. I saw a boy at first, a shy and introverted boy who dared not speak to his comrades, but who felt a confused, a physically demanding longing for the best-looking boys at the school. However, when he approached one too affectionately he was firmly repelled, a second mocked him with cruel clarity, and worse still, the two of them revealed his outlandish desires to the other boys. At

once a unanimous kangaroo court ostracized the confused boy with scorn and humiliation from their cheerful company, as if he were a leper. His way to school
became a daily penance, and his nights were disturbed
by the self-disgust of one marked out early as a pariah,
feeling that his perverse desires, although so far they
featured only in his dreams, denoted insanity and were
a shameful vice.

His voice trembled uncertainly as he told the tale—for
a moment it seemed about to fade away in the darkness.
But a sigh raised it again, and new images rose from the
gloomy haze, ranged one by one, shadowy and ghostly.
The boy became a student in Berlin, and for the first
time the underworld of the city offered him a chance to
satisfy the inclinations he had so long controlled—but
how soiled their satisfaction was by disgust, how poisoned by fear!—those surreptitious encounters on dark
street corners, in the shadows of railway stations and
bridges, how poor a thing was their twitching lust, how
dreadful did the danger make them, most of them end-
ing wretchedly in blackmail and always leaving a slimy
snail-trail of cold fear behind for weeks! The way to hell
lay between darkness and light—while the crystal element of the intellect cleansed the scholar in the bright
light of the industrious day, the evening always impelled
the passionate man towards the dregs of the outskirts
of town, the community of questionable companions

143

avoiding any policeman's spiked helmet, and took him into gloomy beer cellars whose dubious doors opened only to a certain kind of smile. And he had to steel his will to hide this double life with care, to conceal his Medusa-like secret from any strange gaze, to preserve the impeccably grave and dignified demeanour of a junior lecturer by day, only to wander incognito by night in the underworld of shameful adventures pursued by the light of flickering lamps. Again and again the tormented man strained to master a passion which diverged from the accustomed track by applying the lash of self-control, again and again his instincts impelled him towards the dark and dangerous. Ten, twelve, fifteen years of nerve-racking struggles with the invisibly magnetic power of his incurable inclination were like a single convulsion. He felt satisfaction without enjoyment, he felt choking shame, and came to be aware of the dark aspect, timidly concealed in itself, of his fear of his own passions.

At last, quite late, after his thirtieth year, he made a violent attempt to force his life round to the right track. At the home of a relative he met his future wife, a young girl who, vaguely attracted by the mystery clinging about him, offered him genuine affection. And for once her boyish body and youthfully spirited bearing managed, briefly, to deceive his passion. Their fleeting relationship conquered his resistance to all things feminine, he overcame it for the first time, and hoping that thanks to this attraction he would be able to master his misdirected inclinations, impatient to chain himself fast when for once he had found a prop against his inner propensity for the dangerous, and having made a full admission of it to her first, he quickly married the girl. Now he thought the way back to those terrible zones would be barred to him. For a few brief weeks he was carefree, but soon the new stimulus proved ineffective and his original longings became insistent and overpowering. From then on the girl whom he had disappointed and who disappointed him served only as a façade to conceal his revived inclinations. Once again he walked his perilous way on the edge of the law and society, looking down into the dark dangers below.

And a particular torment was added to his inner confusion: he was offered a position where such inclinations as his are a curse. A junior lecturer, who soon became a full professor, he was professionally obliged to be constantly involved with young men, and temptation kept placing new blooms of youth in front of him, ephebes of an invisible *gymnasion* within the world of Prussian conventionality. And all of them—another curse, another danger!—loved him passionately without seeing the face of Eros behind their teacher's mask, they were happy when his comradely but secretly trembling hand touched them, they lavished enthusiasm on a man who had to keep strict control over himself. His were the torments of Tantalus: to be harsh to those who pressed their admiration on him, to fight a never-ending battle with his own weakness! And when he felt that he had almost succumbed to temptation he always suddenly took flight. Those were the escapades whose lightning advent and recurrence had so confused me: now I saw that the terrible way he took was a means of flight from himself, a flight into the horrors of chasms and crooked alleys. He always went to some large metropolis where he would find intimates haunting the wrong side of the tracks, men of the lower classes whose encounters besmirched him, whorish youths instead of young men of elevated and upright minds, but this disgust, this mire, this vileness, this poisonously mordant disappointment was necessary if he were to be sure of resisting the lure of his senses at home, in the close, trusting circle of his students. Ah, what encounters—what ghostly yet malodorously earthly figures his confession conjured up before my eyes! For this distinguished intellectual, in whom a sense of the beauty of form was as natural and necessary as breath, this master of all emotions was fated to encounter ultimate humiliation in low dives, smoky and smouldering, which admitted only initiates; he knew the impudent demands of rent boys with made-up faces, the sugary familiarity of perfumed barbers' assistants, the excited giggling of transvestites in women's skirts, the rabid greed of itinerant

actors, the coarse affection of tobacco-chewing sail-
ors—all these crooked, intimidated, perverse, fantastic
forms in which the sexual instinct, wandering from the
usual way, seeks and knows itself in the meaner areas
of big cities. He had encountered all kinds of humiliation, ignominy and vileness on these slippery paths;
several times he had been robbed of everything on him
(being too weak and too high-minded to scuffle with
a coarse groom), he had been left without his watch,
without his coat, and in addition was spurned by his
drunken comrade when he returned to their shady
hotel on the city outskirts. Blackmailers had got their
claws into him, one of them had dogged his footsteps
at the university for months, sitting boldly in the front
row of the audience and glancing up with a sly smile
at the professor known all over town who, trembling
to see the man's knowing winks, could deliver his lecture only with a great effort. Once—my heart stood
still when he confessed this too—once he had been
picked up by the police in a disreputable bar in Berlin
at midnight with a whole gang of such fellows; a stout,
red-cheeked sergeant took down the trembling man's
name and position with the scornful, superior smile
of a subaltern suddenly able to put on airs in front of
an intellectual, graciously indicating at last that this
time he was being let off with a caution, but hence-
forward his name would be on a certain list. And as a

man who has sat too long in bars that smell of liquor finds its odour clinging at last to his clothes, so rumours and gossip gradually went round here in his own town, beginning in some place that could not be traced; it was the same as in his class at school—in the company of his colleagues their conversation and greetings to him became ostentatiously more and more frosty, until here too a glazed and transparent area of alienation cut the isolated man off from all of them. And even in the safety of his home, behind many locked doors, he still felt he was being spied on and known for what he was.

But this tormented, fearful heart was never offered the grace of pure friendship by a nobly minded man, the worthy return of a virile and powerful affection: he always had to divide his feelings into below and above, his tender longings for his young and intellectual students at the university, and those companions hired in the dark of whom he would think with revulsion next morning. Never, as he began to age, did he experience a pure inclination, a youth's wholehearted affection for him, and weary of disappointment, his nerves worn out by struggling through this thorny thicket, he had resigned himself to the idea that he was done for, when suddenly a young man came into his life who showed a passionate liking for him, ageing as he was, who willingly offered up his words, his whole being, who felt ardently for him—and he, unsuspectingly overwhelmed, now faced in alarm the miracle for which he had no longer hoped, feeling himself unworthy now of such a pure, spontaneously offered gift. Once again a messenger of youth had appeared, a handsome form and a passionate mind burning for him with intellectual fire, affectionately bound to him by a link of sympathy, thirsting for his liking, and with no idea of its own danger. With the torch of Eros in his guileless soul, bold and innocent as Parsifal the holy fool, this youth bent close to the poisoned wound, unaware of his magic or that even his arrival brought healing—it was the boy for whom he had waited so long, for all his life, and who came into it too late, at the last sunset hour.

And as he described this figure his voice rose from the darkness. A lightness seemed to come into it, a deep sound of affection lent it music as that eloquent mouth spoke of the young man, his late-come love. I trembled with excitement and sympathy, but suddenly—my heart was struck as if by a hammer. For that ardent young man of whom my teacher spoke was … was … shame sprang to my cheeks … was I myself: I saw myself step forward as if out of a burning mirror, enveloped in such a radiance of undivined love that its reflection singed me. Yes, I was the young man—more and more closely I recognized myself, my urgent enthusiasm, my fanatical desire to be close to him, the ecstasy of yearning for which the intellect was not enough, I was the foolish, wild boy who, unaware of his power, had roused the burgeoning seeds of creativity once again in the withdrawn scholar, had once again inflamed the torch of Eros in his soul as its weary flame burned low. In amazement I now realized what I, who had felt so timid, meant to him, it was my headlong impetuosity that he loved as the most sacrosanct surprise of his old age—and with a shudder I also saw how powerfully his will had fought with me: for from me of all people, whom he loved purely, he did not want to experience rejection and contempt, the horror of insulted physicality, or see this last grace granted by cruel Fortune made a lustful plaything for the senses. That was why he resisted my persistence so firmly, poured sudden cold water ironically over my overflowing emotions, sharply added a note of conventional rigour to soft and friendly conversations, restrained the hand reaching tenderly out—for my sake alone he forced himself to all the brusque behaviour meant to sober me up and preserve him, conduct which had distressed my mind for weeks. The confused devastation of the night when, in the dream world of his overpowered senses, he had climbed the creaking stair to save himself and our friendship with those hurtful remarks was cruelly clear to me now. And shuddering, gripped, moved as if in a fever, overflowing with pity, I understood how he had suffered for my sake, how heroically he had controlled himself for me.

That voice in the darkness, ah, that voice in the darkness, how I felt it penetrate my inmost breast! There was a note in it such as I had never heard before and have never heard since, a note drawn from depths that the average life never plumbs. A man speaks thus only once in his life to another, to fall silent then for ever, as in the legend of the swan which is said to be capable of raising its hoarse voice in song only once, when it is dying. And I received that fervent, ardently urgent voice pressing on with its tale into me with a shuddering and painful sensation, as a woman takes a man into herself.

Then, suddenly, the voice fell silent, and there was nothing but darkness between us. I knew he was close to me. I had only to lift my hand and reach out to touch him. And I felt a powerful urge to comfort the suffering man.

But then he made a movement. The light came on. Tired, old and tormented, a figure rose from his chair—an exhausted old man slowly approached me. "Goodbye, Roland—not another word between us now! I am glad you came—and we must both be glad that you are going ... goodbye. And—let me kiss you as we say farewell."

As if impelled by some magic power I stumbled towards him. That smouldering light, usually hidden as if by drifting mists, was now glowing openly in his eyes; burning flames rose from them. He drew me close, his lips pressed mine thirstily, nervously, and with a trembling convulsion he held my body close to his.

It was a kiss such as I have never received from a woman, a kiss as wild and desperate as a deathly cry. The trembling of his body passed into me. I shuddered, in the strange grip of a terrible sensation—responding with my soul, yet deeply alarmed by the defensive reaction of my body when touched by a man—I responded with an eerie confusion of feeling which stretched those few seconds out into a dizzying length of time.

Then he let go of me—with a sudden movement as if a body were being violently torn apart—turned with difficulty and threw himself into his chair, his back to me. Perfectly rigid, he leaned forward into the empty air for a few moments. But gradually his head became too heavy, he bent it first more wearily, more dully, and then his brow, like something too weighty swaying for a while and then suddenly falling, dropped to the desktop with a hollow, dry sound.

Infinite waves of pity surged through me. Involuntarily I stepped closer. But then, suddenly, he straightened his bent spine, and as he turned back his hoarse voice, dull and admonitory, groaned from the cup of his clenched hands: "Go away! Go away! Don't … don't come near me … for God's sake, for both our sakes, go now, go!"

I understood. And I retreated, shuddering; I left that beloved room like a man in flight.

I NEVER SAW HIM AGAIN. I never received any letter or message. His work was never published, his name is forgotten; no one else knows anything about him, only I alone. But even today, as once I did when I was a boy still unsure of myself, I feel that I have more to thank him for than my mother and father before him or my wife and children after him. I have never loved anyone more.

PUSHKIN PRESS

Pushkin Press was founded in 1997. Having first rediscovered European classics of the twentieth century, Pushkin now publishes novels, essays, memoirs, children's books, and everything from timeless classics to the urgent and contemporary.

This book is part of the Pushkin Collection of paperbacks, designed to be as satisfying as possible to hold and to enjoy. It is typeset in Monotype Baskerville, based on the transitional English serif typeface designed in the mid-eighteenth century by John Baskerville. It was litho-printed on Munken Premium White Paper and notch-bound by the independently owned printer TJ International in Padstow, Cornwall. The cover, with French flaps, was printed on Colorplan Pristine White paper. The paper and cover board are both acid-free and Forest Stewardship Council (FSC) certified.

Pushkin Press publishes the best writing from around the world—great stories, beautifully produced, to be read and read again.